SO COLD

(A Faith Bold Mystery —Book Two)

BLAKE PIERCE

Blake Pierce

Blake Pierce is the USA Today bestselling author of the RILEY PAGE mystery series, which includes seventeen books. Blake Pierce is also the author of the MACKENZIE WHITE mystery series, comprising fourteen books; of the AVERY BLACK mystery series, comprising six books; of the KERI LOCKE mystery series, comprising five books; of the MAKING OF RILEY PAIGE mystery series, comprising six books; of the KATE WISE mystery series, comprising seven books; of the CHLOE FINE psychological suspense mystery, comprising six books; of the JESSIE HUNT psychological suspense thriller series, comprising twenty-eight books; of the AU PAIR psychological suspense thriller series, comprising three books; of the ZOE PRIME mystery series, comprising six books; of the ADELE SHARP mystery series, comprising sixteen books, of the EUROPEAN VOYAGE cozy mystery series, comprising six books; of the LAURA FROST FBI suspense thriller, comprising eleven books; of the ELLA DARK FBI suspense thriller, comprising fourteen books (and counting); of the A YEAR IN EUROPE cozy mystery series, comprising nine books, of the AVA GOLD mystery series, comprising six books; of the RACHEL GIFT mystery series, comprising ten books (and counting); of the VALERIE LAW mystery series, comprising nine books (and counting); of the PAIGE KING mystery series, comprising eight books (and counting); of the MAY MOORE mystery series, comprising eleven books; of the CORA SHIELDS mystery series, comprising eight books (and counting); of the NICKY LYONS mystery series, comprising eight books (and counting), of the CAMI LARK mystery series, comprising eight books (and counting), of the AMBER YOUNG mystery series, comprising five books (and counting), of the DAISY FORTUNE mystery series, comprising five books (and counting), of the FIONA RED mystery series, comprising five books (and counting), and of the new FAITH BOLD mystery series, comprising five books (and counting).

An avid reader and lifelong fan of the mystery and thriller genres, Blake loves to hear from you, so please feel free to visit www.blakepierceauthor.com to learn more and stay in touch.

ISBN: 978-1-0943-8180-0

BOOKS BY BLAKE PIERCE

FAITH BOLD MYSTERY SERIES
SO LONG (Book #1)
SO COLD (Book #2)
SO SCARED (Book #3)
SO NORMAL (Book #4)
SO FAR GONE (Book #5)

FIONA RED MYSTERY SERIES
LET HER GO (Book #1)
LET HER BE (Book #2)
LET HER HOPE (Book #3)
LET HER WISH (Book #4)
LET HER LIVE (Book #5)

DAISY FORTUNE MYSTERY SERIES
NEED YOU (Book #1)
CLAIM YOU (Book #2)
CRAVE YOU (Book #3)
CHOOSE YOU (Book #4)
CHASE YOU (Book #5)

AMBER YOUNG MYSTERY SERIES
ABSENT PITY (Book #1)
ABSENT REMORSE (Book #2)
ABSENT FEELING (Book #3)
ABSENT MERCY (Book #4)
ABSENT REASON (Book #5)

CAMI LARK MYSTERY SERIES
JUST ME (Book #1)
JUST OUTSIDE (Book #2)
JUST RIGHT (Book #3)
JUST FORGET (Book #4)
JUST ONCE (Book #5)
JUST HIDE (Book #6)

JUST NOW (Book #7)
JUST HOPE (Book #8)

NICKY LYONS MYSTERY SERIES
ALL MINE (Book #1)
ALL HIS (Book #2)
ALL HE SEES (Book #3)
ALL ALONE (Book #4)
ALL FOR ONE (Book #5)
ALL HE TAKES (Book #6)
ALL FOR ME (Book #7)
ALL IN (Book #8)

CORA SHIELDS MYSTERY SERIES
UNDONE (Book #1)
UNWANTED (Book #2)
UNHINGED (Book #3)
UNSAID (Book #4)
UNGLUED (Book #5)
UNSTABLE (Book #6)
UNKNOWN (Book #7)
UNAWARE (Book #8)

MAY MOORE SUSPENSE THRILLER
NEVER RUN (Book #1)
NEVER TELL (Book #2)
NEVER LIVE (Book #3)
NEVER HIDE (Book #4)
NEVER FORGIVE (Book #5)
NEVER AGAIN (Book #6)
NEVER LOOK BACK (Book #7)
NEVER FORGET (Book #8)
NEVER LET GO (Book #9)
NEVER PRETEND (Book #10)
NEVER HESITATE (Book #11)

PAIGE KING MYSTERY SERIES
THE GIRL HE PINED (Book #1)
THE GIRL HE CHOSE (Book #2)
THE GIRL HE TOOK (Book #3)

THE GIRL HE WISHED (Book #4)
THE GIRL HE CROWNED (Book #5)
THE GIRL HE WATCHED (Book #6)
THE GIRL HE WANTED (Book #7)
THE GIRL HE CLAIMED (Book #8)

VALERIE LAW MYSTERY SERIES
NO MERCY (Book #1)
NO PITY (Book #2)
NO FEAR (Book #3)
NO SLEEP (Book #4)
NO QUARTER (Book #5)
NO CHANCE (Book #6)
NO REFUGE (Book #7)
NO GRACE (Book #8)
NO ESCAPE (Book #9)

RACHEL GIFT MYSTERY SERIES
HER LAST WISH (Book #1)
HER LAST CHANCE (Book #2)
HER LAST HOPE (Book #3)
HER LAST FEAR (Book #4)
HER LAST CHOICE (Book #5)
HER LAST BREATH (Book #6)
HER LAST MISTAKE (Book #7)
HER LAST DESIRE (Book #8)
HER LAST REGRET (Book #9)
HER LAST HOUR (Book #10)

AVA GOLD MYSTERY SERIES
CITY OF PREY (Book #1)
CITY OF FEAR (Book #2)
CITY OF BONES (Book #3)
CITY OF GHOSTS (Book #4)
CITY OF DEATH (Book #5)
CITY OF VICE (Book #6)

A YEAR IN EUROPE
A MURDER IN PARIS (Book #1)
DEATH IN FLORENCE (Book #2)

VENGEANCE IN VIENNA (Book #3)
A FATALITY IN SPAIN (Book #4)

ELLA DARK FBI SUSPENSE THRILLER
GIRL, ALONE (Book #1)
GIRL, TAKEN (Book #2)
GIRL, HUNTED (Book #3)
GIRL, SILENCED (Book #4)
GIRL, VANISHED (Book 5)
GIRL ERASED (Book #6)
GIRL, FORSAKEN (Book #7)
GIRL, TRAPPED (Book #8)
GIRL, EXPENDABLE (Book #9)
GIRL, ESCAPED (Book #10)
GIRL, HIS (Book #11)
GIRL, LURED (Book #12)
GIRL, MISSING (Book #13)
GIRL, UNKNOWN (Book #14)

LAURA FROST FBI SUSPENSE THRILLER
ALREADY GONE (Book #1)
ALREADY SEEN (Book #2)
ALREADY TRAPPED (Book #3)
ALREADY MISSING (Book #4)
ALREADY DEAD (Book #5)
ALREADY TAKEN (Book #6)
ALREADY CHOSEN (Book #7)
ALREADY LOST (Book #8)
ALREADY HIS (Book #9)
ALREADY LURED (Book #10)
ALREADY COLD (Book #11)

EUROPEAN VOYAGE COZY MYSTERY SERIES
MURDER (AND BAKLAVA) (Book #1)
DEATH (AND APPLE STRUDEL) (Book #2)
CRIME (AND LAGER) (Book #3)
MISFORTUNE (AND GOUDA) (Book #4)
CALAMITY (AND A DANISH) (Book #5)
MAYHEM (AND HERRING) (Book #6)

ADELE SHARP MYSTERY SERIES
LEFT TO DIE (Book #1)
LEFT TO RUN (Book #2)
LEFT TO HIDE (Book #3)
LEFT TO KILL (Book #4)
LEFT TO MURDER (Book #5)
LEFT TO ENVY (Book #6)
LEFT TO LAPSE (Book #7)
LEFT TO VANISH (Book #8)
LEFT TO HUNT (Book #9)
LEFT TO FEAR (Book #10)
LEFT TO PREY (Book #11)
LEFT TO LURE (Book #12)
LEFT TO CRAVE (Book #13)
LEFT TO LOATHE (Book #14)
LEFT TO HARM (Book #15)
LEFT TO RUIN (Book #16)

THE AU PAIR SERIES
ALMOST GONE (Book#1)
ALMOST LOST (Book #2)
ALMOST DEAD (Book #3)

ZOE PRIME MYSTERY SERIES
FACE OF DEATH (Book#1)
FACE OF MURDER (Book #2)
FACE OF FEAR (Book #3)
FACE OF MADNESS (Book #4)
FACE OF FURY (Book #5)
FACE OF DARKNESS (Book #6)

A JESSIE HUNT PSYCHOLOGICAL SUSPENSE SERIES
THE PERFECT WIFE (Book #1)
THE PERFECT BLOCK (Book #2)
THE PERFECT HOUSE (Book #3)
THE PERFECT SMILE (Book #4)
THE PERFECT LIE (Book #5)
THE PERFECT LOOK (Book #6)
THE PERFECT AFFAIR (Book #7)
THE PERFECT ALIBI (Book #8)

THE PERFECT NEIGHBOR (Book #9)
THE PERFECT DISGUISE (Book #10)
THE PERFECT SECRET (Book #11)
THE PERFECT FAÇADE (Book #12)
THE PERFECT IMPRESSION (Book #13)
THE PERFECT DECEIT (Book #14)
THE PERFECT MISTRESS (Book #15)
THE PERFECT IMAGE (Book #16)
THE PERFECT VEIL (Book #17)
THE PERFECT INDISCRETION (Book #18)
THE PERFECT RUMOR (Book #19)
THE PERFECT COUPLE (Book #20)
THE PERFECT MURDER (Book #21)
THE PERFECT HUSBAND (Book #22)
THE PERFECT SCANDAL (Book #23)
THE PERFECT MASK (Book #24)
THE PERFECT RUSE (Book #25)
THE PERFECT VENEER (Book #26)
THE PERFECT PEOPLE (Book #27)
THE PERFECT WITNESS (Book #28)

CHLOE FINE PSYCHOLOGICAL SUSPENSE SERIES
NEXT DOOR (Book #1)
A NEIGHBOR'S LIE (Book #2)
CUL DE SAC (Book #3)
SILENT NEIGHBOR (Book #4)
HOMECOMING (Book #5)
TINTED WINDOWS (Book #6)

KATE WISE MYSTERY SERIES
IF SHE KNEW (Book #1)
IF SHE SAW (Book #2)
IF SHE RAN (Book #3)
IF SHE HID (Book #4)
IF SHE FLED (Book #5)
IF SHE FEARED (Book #6)
IF SHE HEARD (Book #7)

THE MAKING OF RILEY PAIGE SERIES
WATCHING (Book #1)

WAITING (Book #2)
LURING (Book #3)
TAKING (Book #4)
STALKING (Book #5)
KILLING (Book #6)

RILEY PAIGE MYSTERY SERIES
ONCE GONE (Book #1)
ONCE TAKEN (Book #2)
ONCE CRAVED (Book #3)
ONCE LURED (Book #4)
ONCE HUNTED (Book #5)
ONCE PINED (Book #6)
ONCE FORSAKEN (Book #7)
ONCE COLD (Book #8)
ONCE STALKED (Book #9)
ONCE LOST (Book #10)
ONCE BURIED (Book #11)
ONCE BOUND (Book #12)
ONCE TRAPPED (Book #13)
ONCE DORMANT (Book #14)
ONCE SHUNNED (Book #15)
ONCE MISSED (Book #16)
ONCE CHOSEN (Book #17)

MACKENZIE WHITE MYSTERY SERIES
BEFORE HE KILLS (Book #1)
BEFORE HE SEES (Book #2)
BEFORE HE COVETS (Book #3)
BEFORE HE TAKES (Book #4)
BEFORE HE NEEDS (Book #5)
BEFORE HE FEELS (Book #6)
BEFORE HE SINS (Book #7)
BEFORE HE HUNTS (Book #8)
BEFORE HE PREYS (Book #9)
BEFORE HE LONGS (Book #10)
BEFORE HE LAPSES (Book #11)
BEFORE HE ENVIES (Book #12)
BEFORE HE STALKS (Book #13)
BEFORE HE HARMS (Book #14)

AVERY BLACK MYSTERY SERIES
CAUSE TO KILL (Book #1)
CAUSE TO RUN (Book #2)
CAUSE TO HIDE (Book #3)
CAUSE TO FEAR (Book #4)
CAUSE TO SAVE (Book #5)
CAUSE TO DREAD (Book #6)

KERI LOCKE MYSTERY SERIES
A TRACE OF DEATH (Book #1)
A TRACE OF MURDER (Book #2)
A TRACE OF VICE (Book #3)
A TRACE OF CRIME (Book #4)
A TRACE OF HOPE (Book #5)

PROLOGUE

Andrew grunted as he drove the shovel into the dirt where, a week ago, he'd begun to build the fence separating his backyard from the Baxters. Ron Baxter had been in fine form last night, shouting and cursing at Andrew that it was his responsibility to fence off their properties.

Andrew couldn't resist a chuckle. Ron Baxter was five-foot-three and all of a hundred thirty pounds soaking wet. Andrew was no beefcake, but it would take a little more than a balding little twerp like Ron to intimidate him.

"And yet, here you are building the fence," he muttered to himself.

He heaved a sigh, then drove the shovel back into the earth. The hole was about three feet deep now. He didn't need to dig that deep, but by God, if Ron wanted a fence, he would get a fence. He would get the biggest fence he'd ever seen, and Andrew would get to be free from staring at that little stain all day.

He'd miss staring at Liz, though. Ron Baxter might look like the kid you beat up in high school just because, but Liz looked like she hadn't aged a day after twenty-five. He thought of his own wife, who after twenty years of marriage felt safe enough to allow herself to grow chubby and forgo panties in favor of briefs that rivaled his own in size.

Well, it wasn't like he was ever going to do anything with Liz anyway. Secrets traveled fast in a neighborhood like Cedar Hills.

He drove the shovel again, and this time he heard a crunch under the blade. Maybe he had hit a root or something.

He leaned against the shovel and looked into the hole.

It wasn't a root.

Andrew's blood froze. His stomach turned and his heart leapt to his throat.

"Bonnie?" he called. "Bonnie!"

"What?" his wife shrieked through the open kitchen window.

"Come here a moment," he said.

A moment later, he heard the backyard door slam shut as his wife stomped over to him. "I swear to God, Andrew, if this is some sort of prank, then I'll—"

Her voice trailed off when she saw the twisted hand sticking up from the soil, bent sharply at the wrist where Andrew's shovel had struck it. She lifted her hands slowly to her face, then screamed.

Andrew stared numbly at the rotting hand.

And the first thought that entered his numb mind was: Ron would have to wait for his fence after all.

CHAPTER ONE

Faith Bold tried to move and found she couldn't. She sat in a rickety wooden chair, her arms bound to the arms of the chair and her legs bound to shackles in the floor. The only light came through a single high window in the building where she was. She looked around as much as her position would allow and saw that she was in a barn, empty save for Faith and a moving tray like the ones they had at a dentist's office. The tray held several tools, all of them wicked-looking, all of them rusty, most of them stained brown with dried blood.

The door to the barn opened and a blade of light seared Faith's eyes. She blinked against the assault until the blade disappeared. When she saw who had entered the building, Faith's blood froze.

Jethro Trammell, the Donkey Killer, approached slowly, his eyes gleaming with insanity. He approached Faith and leaned in close, a manic grin splitting his face. Faith's nostrils flared as his sour breath wafted across her face.

He showed her his knife, the blade rusty and pitted save for the edge which was polished and sharpened so that it gleamed in the soft light that filtered through the barn's window. "Let's see how you bleed, little girl," he said.

She wasn't going to scream. She wasn't going to give him that satisfaction. He could hurt her. He could kill her. He could chop her up like a side of beef if he wanted to, but he wasn't going to hear her scream.

Then the knife split her skin just behind her left knee. She heard a soft pop, then another, as her tendons were severed cleanly and her resolve vanished in an ear-splitting shriek of agony.

Faith woke with a start. She felt something rough and wet drag across her cheek and sat up to see Turk standing next to the edge of the bed, regarding her plaintively.

She sighed and reached down to stroke him behind his ears. "Sorry, buddy," she said. "I woke you again, didn't I?"

The nightmares came more often now, ever since Michael told her that another killer was following Trammell's M.O. Each time she had one, Turk was there to wake her. She smiled softly at him and said, "Good dog."

She glanced at her clock. It read four-ten. Her alarm was set for six, but she knew she would get no more sleep tonight. She rolled out of bed and headed to the kitchen to prepare breakfast.

As she ate, she thought of the copycat killer case, the one the Boss refused to give her even though she was the most qualified to work on it. Her own experience with the original Donkey Killer meant she was the one most invested in the case as well. It was a mistake to keep her off of it.

Clark and Desrouleaux had been sympathetic when she asked to look at the case, but they had stopped short of allowing her to read the files. She didn't blame them. If the Boss caught them sharing information with her, it would be the end of their careers, not to mention her own.

She couldn't just let the case go, though. Not with someone out there doing to other people what Trammell had done to her.

She pushed these thoughts from her mind and called to Turk. "Come on, boy. Time to run."

He drank from his water bowl for a few seconds, then snorted and trotted after her.

Their morning run took them in a semi-circuitous route around the urban neighborhood where they lived and cut through a city park before looping back around a boulevard that, in an hour or so, would be packed with commuters but was now relatively quiet.

Today, though, Turk decided he had different plans. When they reached the footpath that would lead them through the park, Turk stopped a moment. Faith ran past him, and when she realized he wasn't following, she stopped and said, "Come on, boy. We're going this way."

Turk put his nose to the ground and tracked a scent for a few feet before popping his head up and staring down the road.

"Leave it," Faith said, thinking that he was tracking a rat or a squirrel. "Come on, boy."

Turk turned to look at her for a moment, then turned to look down the road again. She sighed and jogged back in his direction. "Come on, boy," she said, "I let you run without a leash, but if you're going to start ignoring me when I call, I'm putting it back on."

When she got within a few yards of Turk, he bolted.

"Turk!" she called. "Leave it!"

Turk ran maybe thirty yards ahead before stopping and waiting for Faith to catch up. She did, and he bolted again.

Faith felt frustration rise in her neck, but before she could call out to him again, she stopped herself. He never ran off like this. Maybe he smelled something—drugs or blood or something like that. He was a trained K9 after all. He was conditioned to respond to evidence of a crime.

She followed him, and when Turk realized that she wouldn't try to pull him away, he allowed her to keep pace with him. "Be careful, boy," she called after him. "Keep your distance."

Turk led her out of the residential neighborhood and into a business district with moderately sized office buildings and boutique cafés with semi-charming names such as The Morning Mug, Jenna's Joe, and the HotSpot. The few people out and about cast mildly curious glances at the jogger who for some reason had decided to complete her morning run here with her dog instead of at the park a quarter-mile away.

Turk stopped in front of one of the nicer-looking cafés which bore the charming name of the Cozy Corner and looked triumphantly back at Faith. She sighed and shook her head in mild exasperation. "You want coffee, boy?" she said. "Or a muffin?"

Turk barked, then turned back to the coffee shop. A second later the door opened, and Faith blushed when she understood the reason for Turk's behavior.

Dr. David Friedman's eyes widened when he saw the two of them standing in front of the coffee shop. He looked absolutely perfect in his black, long-sleeved shirt and white uniform pants, his hair perfectly combed in the slightly messy style that all young men these days tried to affect but very few could actually pull off.

David could pull it off. David could absolutely pull it off.

"Hey there," he said, his face lighting up in a smile that elevated his attractiveness from breathtaking to devastating. "Look who it is."

Turk barked happily and trotted up to David, wagging his tail, and leaping into David's arms. Faith felt a moment of gratitude that he at least had left David's face alone.

"What brings you two here?" David asked, looking at Faith while he stroked Turk's fur.

"Oh," Faith said, "Oh, um nothing. Just running."

Her cheeks were on fire. God, why was she so hopelessly tongue-tied around him?

"Gotcha," he says, "That's good. I'm glad to see my favorite patient is getting his exercise."

Turk barked and looked back at Faith. When she remained rooted to the spot, he snorted irritably and trotted over to her, staring expectantly.

Faith kept staring at David, too flummoxed to think of anything else to say. After a moment, David said, "Well, I have to get to work, but I'll see you guys soon, all right? Turk here's due for his vaccines in a few weeks."

He started toward his car, a late-model sedan that was nice but not pretentious and loud like most of the cars that doctors and vets drove. Turk watched him go for a moment, then turned to Faith and barked as if to say, "Hey! What are you doing? Say something, moron!"

Faith blinked and called after David. "Wait!"

He stopped with his hand on the car door and turned to her, lifting an eyebrow.

"Um," Faith began. After a moment of horrifically awkward silence, she blurted out, "Would you like to have coffee?"

David smiled slightly and Faith glanced at the to-go cup of coffee in his hand. "I mean lunch," she said, her cheeks flaming again.

"I would love to," he said. "I would take you up on that today, but I have a full schedule, unfortunately. Flu season's starting soon, and I have a long list of furry friends who need their vaccines. Including you, Turk, so I'd better see your butt in my office in a few weeks or your partner and I are going to have words."

Turk barked firmly, and David laughed. "You hear that?" he told Faith. "Better take care of him or he'll tattle. Anyway, lunch sounds wonderful."

"Yeah," Faith said, "Great. Um…"

Her voice trailed off. She had begun to apologize for blowing him off for dinner last month, but she couldn't bring herself to say the words. Besides, the situation was awkward enough already.

"Yeah," Faith finished lamely. "Great."

David smiled. "Wonderful," he said. "I have your number. When I get a free moment, I'll give you a call."

"Great!" Faith said, wondering if her voice sounded as insane to David as it did to her. "Looking forward to it."

"Me too," David said.

He might only be showing politeness to her. Probably he was only being polite. Still, she felt herself grow hot and cold all over at the implication that he might actually be looking forward to a real date with her. To protect herself from further embarrassment—not that this could get much more embarrassing—she offered what had to be the goofiest wave ever and said, "Well, bye!"

"Goodbye, Faith," David said.

Faith turned and jogged away, her face flaming. Turk jogged after her, and when Faith looked down at him, he wore a smile that was equal parts smug and satisfied. He looked up at Faith and lifted an eyebrow, and Faith giggled.

Oh my God, had she asked a man out? Had she really asked a man out? She couldn't remember the last time she had done that. In fact, she had *never* done that.

She looked down at her self-satisfied companion and said, "Good dog."

Turk looked up at her and nodded, and Faith said, "Let's make this a run instead of a jog. What do you say, you giant, furry matchmaker?"

Turk sure as heck seemed to like the idea. Faith picked up the pace, and as the jog became a run, she felt a wonderful sense of… Well, was it well-being? She couldn't be sure. Her cheeks were still a little hot. She blushed as she thought about David. She felt a lot like a schoolgirl who just mooned over a boy as though her whole world were wrapped up in the attention he might show carrying her books or walking her to her locker. She liked the feeling. "Good dog," she said again, "thank you, boy."

She'd run for about a minute when her phone rang. She glanced at it, intending to reject the call. Instead, when she saw who it was, she slowed to a walk and answered. "Boss?" she asked.

"Why are you breathing hard?"

"I'm in the middle of sex with the pool boy," she said. "What do you think?"

Few people could get away with talking to the Boss like that, but he and Faith were close enough that she could get him with a little sarcasm.

When the Boss didn't respond, Faith worried she might have gone too far after all. She said, "I'm just out for a run with the dog. What's up?"

"Well, run back to the house and suit up. We need you."

"What's up?"

"Bodies. Move your butt," he said, and the line went dead.

CHAPTER TWO

Bodies. Not a body. More than one.

She considered calling him back for more information but instead, she jogged back home and took a quick shower. She felt an odd mix of excitement about a new case and irritation that he was assigning her something new instead of giving her the case she wanted. As she dried off, her phone chimed and she walked to where she'd tossed it on the bed. Michael. He was ten minutes from her place.

She dressed quickly and made a fresh pot of coffee while she waited for him. Michael was notorious for being particular about his coffee, and she decided to be nice and make him some of the heirloom coffee she bought from another of those hipster coffee shops a few days ago.

She knew but didn't quite admit to herself that the reason for this extra attention was that she would eventually call on Michael to help her investigate the case she wasn't supposed to look at, and she wanted to ingratiate herself to him.

Turk didn't bark. She didn't know how he could tell from a knock if the man at the door was a man she welcomed or a stranger. Somehow, he managed to do that, though. Smell maybe? Who knew? She got up and answered and Michael raised an eyebrow immediately. "What are you so happy about?"

Dear Lord, she hadn't lost her goofy, schoolgirl grin. "Can't I be happy to see my partner?" she asked. "I made you coffee."

"What do you want?" Michael asked. He didn't return her smile.

"Oh my God, what's gotten into you?" she asked, keeping her smile. "I'm just glad to see you. Ever since you started dating Ellie, it's like I don't exist."

Michael rolled his eyes, but he finally smiled and accepted the coffee. "Hey, we had good times, Faith," he began.

This time it was Faith's turn to roll her eyes. "Don't ruin it," she said.

Michael's grin widened and he said, "I'll always think fondly on the time we shared. A part of me will always love you. You'll always be my first."

She looked frankly at him. "I was your first?"

"No," he said, "just my fondest. Until Ellie, at least."

"And on that awkward note," she said, rolling her eyes again and pushing past him into the hallway.

Michael laughed. "Hey, you brought it up."

"I brought Ellie up," she said, "I didn't say anything about ancient history."

Michael and Faith had dated once upon a time. They broke up about a year before the Donkey Killer case, and things were naturally awkward between the two of them for a while. The awkwardness was gone now, but they both teased each other semi-regularly about it. Faith supposed it helped remind both of them that things were okay between them now.

"Any idea what this case is about?" she asked once they were in the car.

"No idea," Michael said. "Two bodies. That's all I know."

"I knew bodies but not how many," she said.

"Two so far," Michael repeated. "As far as multiple bodies go, that's as good of news as we can get. How's the mutt?"

"I think he has plans of his own," she said, "You know what he did this morning?" She regretted the question the moment it was out of her mouth. She didn't want to tell Michael about David. She wasn't worried about jealousy, especially not now that Michael was dating too, but she didn't want to risk Michael doing something embarrassing like making an excuse to meet David and play the responsible caring partner by grilling him about his past or running him through NICBCS or something.

"What?" Michael asked.

"He woke me up. He wanted to run and he just woke me up. I wasn't going to jog today but I did." There were so many lies in that beyond omitting the part about David, and she felt a slight stab of guilt. He woke her up from a nightmare about Trammell, and she absolutely intended to jog this morning. She didn't like that she was lying to Michael, partly because she knew he would never lie to her and partly because she knew he wouldn't be fooled for long.

"Looks like he gets what he wants when he wants it," Michael chuckled.

"This morning was a moment of weakness," Faith replied. "He better not get used to it."

Her phone rang. "It's the Boss," she said.

When she answered, he asked, “Where are you?” before she could speak.

“We’re on our way to the office, all three of us.”

“Good,” he said, “make it snappy.”

The Boss hung up and Faith turned to Michael, eyebrow raised.

“He sounded strange on the phone,” Michael offered. “Bodies. This isn’t cut and dry.” Michael didn’t go so far as to say it but if he’d said the words audibly, Faith didn’t think they would have been any louder.

Another serial killer.

They reached the office a few minutes later, and when the security guard saw Michael’s ID, he waved them through without making them stop. A few minutes after that, the three of them were in the Boss’s office.

As usual, he wasted no time getting to the point.

“Two bodies,” he said, “Found this morning in the Cedar Hills community outside of Bryn Mawr.”

Faith’s eyes widened. Cedar Hills was an upscale community, solidly upper-middle-class and near-wealthy.

“Guess it’s not as nice as it looks,” Michael said, echoing Faith’s thoughts.

“You think that’s funny, Prince?” the Boss snapped.

Michael blinked and shook his head.

Faith watched the Boss’s face and saw far more anxiety than she expected to see. Murders were never fun, especially this close to home, but the Boss had been in the FBI since Faith was drawing stick figures with crayons. It was unlike him to be so frazzled by a case.

“Have they identified the bodies yet?” she asked.

“Not yet,” he said. “Did you not hear what I said? They were found this morning a few hours ago.”

“I heard you,” Faith said. “I’m just wondering why they’re already calling us. Unless those victims were murdered out of state and transported here or the police suspect some sort of political or organized crime motive, it’s strange that they would call us right away.”

“The DA is personal friends with Deputy Director Smythe,” the Boss said. “He called in a favor. Turns out his uncle lives in Cedar Hills.”

Ah. That was why the Boss was irritable. He and Deputy Director Smythe had a falling out about ten years ago. The result was that the Boss would never rise above SAC and Smythe probably couldn’t count on a congratulatory phone call from the Boss when he retired. If this was personal to Smythe, it meant dealing with nagging phone calls and emails from him until it was solved.

"Sorry about that," Michael said.

"Thank you for the sympathy, Prince," the Boss snapped. "If I want more, I'll make sure to ask anyone but you. You two—" he glanced at Turk, "—you three are going to Cedar Hills."

"Do we have an address?" Michael asked.

"15843 Oak Crest Drive," the Boss said. "It's a cul-de-sac that backs up to the golf course that all of those communities feel a need to have. The bodies were found by the homeowners. At the moment, we don't suspect them of involvement, but since we don't even know who the victims are yet, we're not ruling anything out."

"Who called it in?" Faith asked. "The homeowners?"

"Bingo," the Boss said. "Give the lady a prize. Apparently, the husband was digging holes for a new fence and struck gold."

"Anyone else see the bodies?" Michael asked.

"Probably," the Boss said. "It's the goddamn Real Housewives out there. This is probably the biggest neighborhood news since the last time one of them screwed the pool boy. Police are on scene, but I guarantee they're spending all their time keeping looky-loos off the property. You three are going to have to move fast."

"Fair enough," Faith said, standing up. "Anything else we should know?"

"Yeah," the Boss said. "Prince, take the dog and beat it. I need to talk to Bold."

Michael raised an eyebrow and looked at Faith. Faith nodded, and Michael took Turk's leash and led him outside. Turk resisted a moment, but when Faith said, "Go on, boy. I'll see you in a minute," he allowed Michael to lead him outside of the office.

When the door closed behind them, the Boss turned to Faith. "Back off," he said.

Faith blinked in confusion. "Sir?"

"The copycat case," he said. "Back off."

Oh.

Faith felt a rush of anger. Clark and Desrouleaux must have told the Boss she was asking about the case. She could understand their reluctance to let her make copies, but they didn't need to tattle on her like that.

"I was just talking to them," Faith said, "I wanted them to know I'm available if they have any questions."

"You're not available," the Boss said. "It's not your case."

"Boss—" she began.

"You still have nightmares, Bold?" the Boss interrupted.

Faith felt as though she had been slapped. She blinked twice and didn't respond.

"Thought so," the Boss said. "You're off that case, Bold. You're a damned fine agent, and I need you healthy and focused."

"I'm healthy," she said. "I passed my psych eval. I'm good to go."

"You passed your psych eval after the Missouri case," the Boss said. "You think you'll pass one now if IA finds out you've been snooping on this case?"

Faith didn't respond. If the Boss knew about her nightmares, then it meant that the way this case affected her showed, and that meant it was even odds at best that she would pass another psych eval. If she failed, it meant an automatic suspension and probably a desk job when she was reassigned.

"Back off," the Boss repeated, "I mean it. You're a good agent. You really are, and I've said that twice in the same conversation, so that should tell you I really mean it. Don't throw away your career over this. Clark and Desrouleaux are good agents too. They'll get this guy."

Faith thought of asking if they would get this guy before he got another half-dozen victims. She thought of asking if the Boss's real reason for giving them this new case was just to occupy her and not because the Deputy Director was involved. The Boss knew the DA too, and he was owed favors as well. He could have convinced the DA to give the Bureau the case just to keep Faith's nose out of the Donkey Killer's case.

She dismissed that line of reasoning as obsessive, but she was still too angry to offer anything other than a clipped, "Understood. Anything else?"

"No," the Boss said, "but please don't die on this hill, Bold. It's not worth it."

Faith nodded and left the office without saying anything else.

The Boss could say it wasn't worth it, but he hadn't been strapped to a chair and butchered alive like Faith had. He hadn't nearly lost his will to live; Faith had. Maybe this copycat killer was just another case to him, but it wasn't to Faith. That's why she was the best choice for the case. That's also why the Boss saw her as the worst choice for the case. From his perspective, she was too emotionally involved. From her perspective, she had the drive and knowledge to solve it before anyone else got hurt.

That was why, when they got to the car, she said to Michael, "Shoot. Wait a second. Forgot something," and ran upstairs.

Clark and Desrouleaux were out to lunch right now. They were predictable as clockwork. They were at French's Deli stuffing their faces with pastrami and sauerkraut, and the case file was exactly where Faith knew it would be, sitting on top of Desrouleaux's desk.

She glanced in the direction of the Boss's office, but he was focused on his computer screen and from where he sat, he wouldn't be able to see Faith unless he intentionally craned his neck and looked at Desrouleaux's desk.

She walked to the copier, keeping her movements nonchalant so as not to arouse suspicion from the other agents. She made a single copy of the case, using the lowest resolution setting to make the copy as quickly as possible. The copy came out grainy and furry, but Faith's eyes were sharp, and she could still read the text easily.

She took the original back to Desrouleaux's desk and took the copy to her own desk. She opened the locked drawer on the bottom of her filing cabinet and set it somewhere in the middle of the paperwork there. She locked the cabinet and headed to the breakroom, getting two cups of coffee before heading back downstairs.

Michael was leaning against his car when she reached him. "What the hell were you doing?" she asked.

Faith lifted the coffee cups in response. "Had to make a new pot."

"You went upstairs to make a pot of shitty coffee?" Michael asked.

"Turk woke me up early, remember?" she explained. "Besides, I like the coffee. Now do you want your cup or not?"

Michael glanced at the cup, and after a second of deliberation, took it from Faith's outstretched hand. "Shit coffee's better than no coffee, I guess."

They got into the car and Michael pulled out of the space and out of the garage. As he turned onto the road, Faith caught Turk staring at her from the middle of the second row of the SUV. It might have been her imagination, but he looked as though he knew what she had really been up to.

She looked away from him and stared out the window until the guilt faded and her mind turned back to the task at hand.

CHAPTER THREE

Michael glanced over at Faith. She stared out the window at nothing. A shadow fell across her left eye, cast by a lock of hair that never quite seemed to fall into place. Michael smiled softly at that shadow. At one time, it had been the most beautiful thing he had ever seen.

He had been in love with Faith once. He supposed a part of him always would be. He had been teasing Faith earlier, but that didn't mean what he said wasn't true. For a moment, he had envisioned a future with her in a nice little house with a picket fence and yard, two kids and a dog, all of that stereotypical stuff.

He no longer envisioned that future, and to be honest, he didn't truly miss his relationship with her. They had both moved on, and he was happy to be her friend and partner and nothing more. Besides, Ellie felt like the real deal. It would be a while before her divorce was finalized and they could truly be together, but she seemed to understand Michael in ways no one, not even Faith, ever had.

Still, when the light fell over Faith's face the way it did now, he remembered how it felt to be in love with her. Love left scars, and those scars never fully healed.

She caught him staring and said, "Something on your mind, Prince?"

"Yeah," he said, "I'm hurt."

She turned to face him, lifting an eyebrow. "You're hurt?"

"I am," he said. "You've hurt me."

"Michael, what the hell are you talking about?" she asked.

"I thought we were friends," he said.

"We are at the moment, but if you don't start talking sense, that's going to change," she replied.

"I'm just saying," he said, "I told you about Ellie the day I met her. You still haven't told me you have the hots for Turk's vet."

She recoiled in shock, her eyes and mouth dropping open wide. "I didn't… I don't… how?"

Michael grinned. "Oh come on, Faith. The day after Turk's appointment, you were prancing and giggling like it was prom night.

This morning when I picked you up, you had the same moon-faced expression. You have a crush. Admit it."

"I don't have to admit anything to you!" she cried.

"See?" he said. "That's why I'm hurt. I told you; you didn't tell me."

"Well, I guess I'm more of a gentleman than you," she retorted, "because I don't kiss and tell."

"So you've kissed him?" Michael asked.

"No!" Faith cried.

Michael laughed and tried not to notice how attractive Faith was when there was color in her face. He supposed he was over her, but there were times when he wondered if he was really over her or just resigned to the reality that he would never have her again. True, he was the one to put the final nail in that coffin, but the relationship was over long before he called the time of death. That ship had sailed. The train had left the station. There were probably a hundred other idioms.

Still, he didn't want to push her, and his feelings for Ellie grew stronger by the day. These moments would occur less and less often and, eventually, they would stop altogether.

"Anyway, as long as you're already more of a gentleman than me," he said, "I guess I ought to tell you that I'm already thinking about this girl as something more than just a passing, casual thing."

"Really?" she asked. "That was quick."

He shrugged. She was probably right about that. "Maybe if we were college kids or something," he said, "but we're not. She's getting over a failed marriage and I'm not getting any younger. You know, when you're a kid, you're looking for a boyfriend or, I guess if you're a guy, you're looking to get laid regularly. When you're older, you go on every date wondering if they're the one."

"Marriage material," Faith said.

"Exactly. You don't want to waste any time."

"So, is this girl, Ellie, marriage material?"

"I think she might be," Michael said. This was a good conversation. Already the wistful remnants of longing for Faith seemed far less wistful and hope for a future with Ellie seemed far stronger.

"Okay, Romeo," Faith said, "why?"

"Why what? Why is she marriage material?"

"What the hell else are we talking about?" she asked.

He chuckled. It was a good question. "Well, she's beautiful."

Faith groaned. "Got it. So that's the key. How in the world do all those porn starlets stay single? Why aren't all those supermodels engaged?" As they drove past a gas station, a woman was standing at the pump. Faith pointed and said, "That blonde there. She looks like marriage material."

Michael said, "All right, all right. I get your point. Let me expand on mine."

"By all means, Casanova," she said sarcastically, "talk your way out of this one."

"She's beautiful to me. I'm attracted to her. I'm not talking about her body, either, though I'm attracted to that. I mean her smile and her eyes. I find her beautiful and I find her most beautiful when we're having a conversation."

"You're not doing a good job of talking your way out of this one," Faith said. She wore an amused smile and he felt like things had turned around. He'd intended to tease her but now he was on the receiving end.

"Yeah," he said, "Well I guess it's possible I'm just a misogynist pig. She's marriage material because she's good sexual stock. You got me. It's all about the sex for me and not her personality. To tell the truth, if she couldn't string three words together, she's hot enough that I'd still be ready to slide a ring on her finger. You win. I can't ever hide anything from you."

"And don't you forget it," Faith said with a laugh, sealing her victory in the exchange.

Michael intended to get back to teasing her about the veterinarian but just then they reached the entrance to the subdivision. "Through this gate or the one on the other side?"

"Either way," she said. "The house in question is right in the middle so it doesn't really matter."

He pulled into the subdivision and immediately let out a whistle. It didn't look like the Real Housewives here. It looked like the upper-middle-class version of the opening scene to Edward Scissorhands. The perfectly manicured lawns, the only slightly varied profiles of the houses, and the consistent color schemes were jarring rather than inviting. The sameness seemed overwhelming to him.

"How in the world would you even recognize your house without the numbers?" he said. "Geez, even the cars all look the same."

He dwelt on that thought for a moment. He hated that all new cars had the same soft, rounded look. He remembered back when it was easy to tell a Ford from a Chevy and a Mercedes from a Toyota.

"Ain't that America?" Faith asked.

"Not my America," Michael said.

"No, the song. Isn't that the one that talks about little pink houses?"

"Oh yeah." He chuckled. "Here we are, everyone with the big American dream. I'm just waiting for the robot wives to show up."

"Robot wives?"

"Seriously?" he asked. "You remember that song but not the movie?"

"Never mind," she said pointing ahead, "it's time to put on your big girl FBI panties."

She pointed to three police cars that seemed to him like an open sore on the plastic surgery perfected flesh of the subdivision. They were parked (not in spaces, of course) in a little recessed parking lot next to a small grass area with a bench in the middle of the first block.

"Open spaces," he said.

"Amenities everywhere," she said. "You think they all look the same, too?"

"It's like a horror show," he said. "But anyway, do we go to the scene directly or check in with these guys?"

"Let's talk to them first," she said, "and get the lay of the land."

As he pulled into an actual parking space, he said, "Can you imagine what living in a place like this does to a person? It's like the entire subdivision is like my grandmother's house. She has those plastic covers on the couches, you know. I'd be afraid to walk on my own driveway without wiping my feet first."

He turned the engine off and said, "You want to take point here or me?"

She shrugged and said, "I will, I guess. For all we know, some of those deputies are hot. You might decide the sheriff is marrying material."

"If he is, you can be my best man."

Faith chuckled and despite his best efforts not to, Michael wondered if she was jealous. He wasn't too pleased to find that part of him hoped she was.

They approached the scene and Michael saw the officers standing around talking with their arms crossed. Either the scene had already been combed through as much as PD felt necessary or else these were the officers who drew the short sticks and were told to stay out of the way.

One of the officers turned at their approach and Faith flashed her badge. "FBI," she said, "I'm Special Agent Bold, this is Special Agent Prince and my K9 unit, Turk. Can we talk to the senior officer on scene, please?"

Michael suppressed a smile at the brief look of surprise that flashed across the uniform's face. They were far enough into the twenty-first century that people born at the start of it were preparing for their second presidential vote, but female authority still shocked some men.

Fortunately, this particular alpha-male was enough a student of the times that he instantly dismissed his shock and answered Faith's question. "That would be the sheriff," he said. "He's in the clubhouse on the other side of the park talking with the sergeant."

Michael's eyes widened.

"Sheriff?" Faith asked. "This is a county investigation?"

The uniform shrugged. "I guess it's your investigation now."

Faith shared a look with Michael, then nodded to the officer. The uniform returned a respectful nod of his own, then promptly went back to caring as little as possible.

Maybe that was unfair. After all, he was right. This was an FBI investigation now, and an overzealous police officer could be more detrimental to a Bureau case than an under-zealous one.

They crossed the field toward a small building that looked like a rotunda except that instead of being left opened, it was enclosed. Inside, a large man in a hat with a ridiculously large five-pointed star was talking to an even larger man with a mustache that covered his entire mouth and moved like a caterpillar as he spoke.

Faith walked in without knocking, Turk at her side, and Michael followed. Mustache cast an irritated look at the three of them, but when he realized who they were, he adopted a similar expression of "screw it," as the officers had in the parking lot.

The sheriff betrayed no such emotion. He stood and extended a hand toward Faith. "Sheriff Morton," he said, shaking first Faith's hand, then Michael's, nodding at Turk, who barked formally. Evidently the sheriff didn't share the police department's latent chauvinism.

"Detective Sergeant Anglesey," Mustache offered.

"Special Agent Bold," Faith replied. "This is my partner, Special Agent Prince and my K9 unit, Turk."

“Pleasure to meet you agents,” Morton said. He turned to the sergeant and said, “We’ll wrap this up later. Go ahead and tell your boys they can head home. The looky-loos have already lost interest. If we need anything, we’ll call you.”

“What about the homeowners?” the sergeant asked. “Should we bring them in for questioning?”

Morton shook his head. “No, that’s all right. I imagine the agents will want to talk to them after they look at the scene. I’m pretty sure they’re telling us the truth anyway.”

“What truth is that?” Faith asked.

“That they don’t know anything,” Anglesey answered, “And the sheriff’s probably right. They don’t look the type.”

They rarely do, Michael thought. He didn’t say the thought out loud, though, and after a brief handshake for each of the FBI agents, Anglesey left to wrangle his officers.

“Well,” Morton said, “Guess we might as well get this road on the show.”

He offered the turn of phrase without a hint of humor. As they left the clubhouse, Michael tried to form an opinion of Morton. He seemed just as passionless as the officers but carried himself with a professional dignity and walked with an energy surprising for his size and age. His eyes were likewise sharp and while his tone may seem bored, Michael decided that was probably not a true reflection of his feelings but rather a result of long years of suppressing his emotions to lull suspects and witnesses into a state of calm.

Overall, he decided he liked the sheriff. He was definitely an improvement over the sheriff in Morgan County, Missouri, who while nice enough as a person could have had his picture next to the word incompetent.

Turk seconded Michael’s opinion by trotting up next to the sheriff and keeping pace with him as they made their way to the scene. The sheriff led them down one of those winding concrete paths designed to make the residents feel like there was more open space than it seemed--a touch of overkill, Michael thought. As they walked, Morton talked.

“Homeowners called at eight-thirty in the morning,” Morton said. “The husband was digging holes for a new fence the neighbors were harassing them to put up. He saw the body and called his wife to make sure he wasn’t going insane. Too bad for everyone his sanity is perfectly intact.”

"If he was digging holes for a fence, then the body would have had to be buried very close to the surface."

"Going theory is that the rains could have pushed it closer to the surface," Morton said, "but that's just spit-balling."

"How long ago was the body buried?" Faith asked.

"Coroner estimates no more than a few days."

"That's too recently for rains to have pushed it to the surface," Michael said. "If it was a shallow grave, then it started as a shallow grave."

"How did the homeowners not notice the body being buried on their property?" Faith asked.

"The story they gave is that they were fishing with the husband's brother upstate. Came home the day before yesterday."

"How convenient," Michael said drily.

The sheriff shrugged. "It checks out. The brother confirmed the story when we called him and Fish and Game has transactions that match the husband's credit card. You guys can follow up again if you like, but I think our homeowners are not the guys."

They crested a small hill—another ubiquitous design element of not-quite-wealthy neighborhoods like this one—and Michael saw the scene. As promised, a flurry of men and women in white coats were combing over a ten-by-fifteen-foot cordoned section of a fenceless yard behind one of the McMansions.

Michael shared a look with Faith, and she offered him a brief smile. He returned one of his own and felt the old excitement grow once more. They might not be lovers anymore, but they were damned good agents. Whoever decided to screw up and bury a body in a backyard had better count their days.

CHAPTER FOUR

Faith followed Morton to the scene, stepping under the cordon and approaching the hole. The hole was now three feet wide by six feet long and about three feet deep. The body was female and only just starting to decompose. The victim was in her forties and wearing a dress that was expensive but not absurdly so, probably not off the rack but not much beyond it. She looked exactly like the kind of woman who would live in a neighborhood like this. Other than the decomposition and the caved in forehead, that is.

Turk approached the body, sniffing, but keeping a respectable distance from it and the CSI investigators who still flitted around. One of the CSIs, a striking woman with brilliant red hair and thick, round glasses, smiled and waved at him, earning one of Turk's formal barks of greeting in return.

"A resident?" Faith asked, nodding toward the victim.

"Probably," Morton responded. "There's no ID on the body. Once the autopsy is completed, we'll reach out and see if we can get an ID."

"Cause of death?"

Morton gestured to the massive blunt-trauma injury on the victim. "Guess."

"Fair enough," Faith responded. "Are we sure that's not postmortem, though?"

"We're not sure of anything yet," Morton replied.

Faith glanced at him, but he showed no sign of anger or frustration. "Anything we should know about the scene? Any evidence?"

"Forensics found a wedding ring," Morton said. "I'll let you talk to them for details."

"What about the other body?" Faith asked. "Anything there?"

"Coroner's assistant took that body already. That one was found near the golf course. Landscapers called it in twenty minutes after this one. Male, mid-forties, Caucasian. No homeowners to deal with there, so we were able to get that body wrapped up and taken to the morgue already. Coroner has the details if you want to talk to him,"

"We'll get there," Faith said. "For now, we'll focus on this victim. However, do we know of any relationship between the victims?"

“Not that we know of,” Morton replied. He checked his watch. “I hate to take off so soon, but I should get back to the office and get ahold of PR. The DA’s gonna want me to prepare a statement. If you need anything else, Special Agent, feel free to call my office. I’m sure we’ll be seeing plenty of each other over the next few weeks.”

Faith couldn’t tell if he was eager, annoyed, or indifferent to that fact. She nodded and he returned a nod of his own and one for Michael and Turk before heading out.

Michael stepped closer and whispered, “What’s your read on him?”

“Not sure,” she said. “You?”

“I like him,” he said. “I just don’t know if he likes us.”

“No one likes us, Michael,” she said.

“That’s not true,” Michael said. “They love us in Morgan County, Missouri.”

“I stand corrected,” Faith said.

She walked to a thinly built man around their age who wore a coat with blue stitching above his left breast that announced him as J. Cantor, Coroner.

“Mr. Cantor?” she said.

Cantor turned to her and smiled. “James, please,” he said, shaking her hand exuberantly. “It’s a pleasure to meet you, Miss Bold. Er, I mean, Special Agent Bold.”

He blushed prettily, and Faith smiled softly before saying, “Can you tell us what you’ve found so far?”

“Well,” he said, scratching his head. “Not much, I’m afraid. The victim is female in her early forties, Caucasian, with green eyes and sandy brown hair. Five-foot-eight, maybe a hundred twenty pounds. Cause of death is almost certainly the caved-in skull, although we’ll need to do an autopsy to confirm it. She was married, but the ring either slipped off after she was buried or was removed and then tossed in with her. We dusted for prints, but it’s been underground for too long to yield anything.”

“Any idea why she was found so close to the surface?” Faith asked.

“Well, you’ll have to talk to CSI for the full picture, but from what they told me, it looks like she was buried just three feet or so under the surface.”

“Why so shallow?” Faith asked.

Cantor lifted his arms and shrugged. Faith nodded, “Right. CSI. And who might that be?”

"Priest is the lead investigator," Cantor said. "Her real name's Ashley Baker, but we call her Priest because she's devout Catholic. Wears a rosary and everything."

"You didn't want to call her Nun?" Michael offered.

Cantor's eyes widened as though he had just learned about the moon landing for the first time. "Huh," he said, "that would have made way more sense."

"Could you point her out to me, please?" Faith asked.

"No need," a crisp voice answered.

The striking redhead from earlier strode toward Faith with an aggressively businesslike expression, extending her hand and saying, "Hi. CSI Baker. The boys call me Priest but…" she looked at Michael and said, "You can call me whatever you want."

Faith suppressed a smile. "Sorry to be the one to tell you this, but Special Agent Prince is taken."

"Shame," Baker said.

Turk barked for attention, and she turned to him and said, "What about this handsome man?"

Faith didn't suppress her smile this time. "Taken as well, I'm afraid."

"All the good ones are," Baker lamented. Her voice adopted its businesslike tone once more, and she said, "The soil here is just over three feet deep. You can't see it from where you're standing, but just underneath that is poured cement. We think it's part of a shared foundation."

"A shared foundation?" Michael asked incredulously.

"Yes," Baker confirmed. "Oftentimes, neighborhoods like this will have shared foundations between multiple homes that extend into the landscaping. It protects against erosion due to weather events and lowers the maintenance requirements."

"Why would they want to save money on maintenance?" Michael asked. "They clearly aren't wanting for funds."

"It's not about the money," Faith answered. "In a neighborhood like this, appearance is everything."

Michael looked at the body still resting in the dirt where it was buried. "Not the best appearance for the neighborhood, is it?"

Baker smiled. "Everyone has secrets buried somewhere, Special Agent."

"That they do," Michael agreed.

"So she was buried shallow because there was no choice. Why here, though?"

"That's outside of my job," Baker replied. "You could try talking to the homeowners. They're inside right now with a couple of uniforms."

"I thought all the uniforms went home," Faith said.

"Sergeant Brick House left a couple to make sure the homeowners don't try to get their stories straight. Going theory is they aren't the perps, but Brick House has always been the suspicious type."

"Can I assume that by Brick House you mean Anglesey?" Faith asked.

"That's the one," Baker confirmed. "We used to call him Shithouse, you know, because he's built like a brick shithouse, but he didn't take too kindly to that."

"Can't imagine why," Michael said drily.

Baker flashed him a stunning smile, and Michael flushed and turned away.

"I understand you found a wedding ring," Faith said. "May I see it?"

"You can look, but you can't touch," Baker said. "Until it's processed, it's my evidence, not yours."

She motioned to one of the CSIs, a young man who looked like he didn't need a razor to maintain his clean shave. He shuffled over and handed Baker a small plastic bag with a tarnished wedding ring. The ring was a plain gold band with no identifying marks that—wait.

"Would you mind?" Faith asked Baker. "I think I see something etched into the underside of the band."

Baker lifted the bag and peered at the mark Faith was talking about. "Well, how about that?" she said.

She reached into her pocket and handed Faith a latex glove.

"No glove, no love," she said. She glanced at Michael and said, "Right, Special Agent Prince?"

Michael reddened and cleared his throat and Faith suppressed another smile as she put on the glove. She pulled the ring carefully from the bag and looked at the mark etched into the band. They were initials. The ring was tarnished enough that the initials weren't perfectly clear, but Faith could make out a DV and either EV or BV.

She held the ring up so Michael could take a picture with his phone, then placed the ring carefully back in the bag. Baker zipped it up and Faith said, "Thank you. We'll go talk to the homeowners now."

"Good luck," Baker offered. She flashed another movie star smile at Michael and said, "If you need anything else, call me."

"Noted," Michael said wryly.

They left the scene and walked through the perfectly manicured lawn toward the house. "Be nice," Faith said when they were out of earshot of Baker, elbowing Michael in the ribs. "She's just teasing you."

"I was nice!" he said, "What should I have done, given her my number?"

"I wonder how Ellie would feel if she knew you were entertaining the hot CSI?" Faith wondered aloud.

"Well, now I know I'm right not to introduce you two," Michael said.

Faith laughed. "Oh stop, you grumpy Gus. I'm just teasing you."

"Awful lot of that going around," Michael said.

"Get used to it," Faith replied.

They reached the house and through the sliding glass door, Faith could see the homeowners sitting at the table while two bored-looking uniforms lounged inside. One of them opened the door for the agents and Faith said, "All right boys. Go ahead and get out of here. We'll take over."

The officers nodded with evident relief and after perfunctory farewells to the homeowners left through the back door.

When they were gone, Faith introduced herself and Michael. The homeowners—Bonnie and Andrew Milton—were once more a perfect stereotype of an upper-middle-class white couple. Bonnie was in her early forties, five-foot-five, and if she was an ounce over a hundred pounds, Faith would retire on the spot. She had dyed red hair that showed her natural nutbrown at the roots and wore dangling pearl earrings. Andrew was maybe ten years older than his wife, barrel-chested, five-foot-ten with a stocky build, and receding hair that he didn't bother to change from gray. He wore a designer polo shirt that probably cost more than Faith's entire uniform and the ubiquitous cargo shorts over long socks and golf shoes.

Both wore the vacant, shellshocked expressions of soldiers who'd just survived their first taste of combat. Faith knew that look, although in her case it came from an actual taste of combat. Not that she judged them for it. She doubted that any trauma in their lives up until now could compare to the shock of seeing a dead woman, probably a neighbor, buried in their backyard.

After the introductions, Faith asked, "May we sit?"

Andrew gestured to the two empty chairs around the table and Faith and Michael sat. Once seated, Faith said, "All right, Mr. Milton. Tell me what happened."

Andrew sighed and wiped sweat from his forehead. When he spoke, his voice was flat with shock rapidly fading to exhaustion. "Well, I was working on digging posts for the fence I'm gonna put up, and I got carried away and dug a little deeper than I needed to. I uncovered a hand and called my wife to make sure I wasn't going crazy." He chuckled bitterly. "Kinda wish I was."

"When did you call the police?" Michael asked.

"Right after we saw… saw the body," Bonnie said, her voice trembling. "I… I ran to the kitchen to get my cell phone and called them, and we've been here ever since. Do you know who she is? Oh God, to think something like that could happen *here.*"

Turk walked to her and laid his head on her lap. Faith nearly called him back, but when Bonnie stroked his fur and visibly relaxed, she decided to let him stay.

"The coroner is still working on an official ID," Faith said, "But if you have an idea who it could be, I would love to hear your thoughts."

"I don't know," Bonnie said, shaking her head and fiddling with her ring.

Faith noticed that. It could be simple nerves, most likely was simple nerves—like the sheriff had said, these two didn't look the type—but she decided to ask about the ring anyway.

"Do the initials EV mean anything to you?"

Andrew shrugged. "Electric vehicle?"

"What about BV?" she asked. "Or DV?"

"I'm sorry," Bonnie said, "I don't know. Are those initials?"

"Yes," Faith said, "We found a wedding band near the victim with the initials DV and EV or possibly BV. Are you sure you don't know anyone by that name?"

Bonnie shook her head. "I'm sorry, no." She turned to her husband. "Drew, do you know a DV?"

He sighed. "Daniel Vargas from high school, but he lives in New Mexico now and his wife looks a little different than our dead body if you know what I mean."

"We don't know what you mean," Michael replied. "Please enlighten us."

"He's a guy," Drew said. "Daniel's gay." He rubbed his forehead again. "Sorry, I shouldn't have said it like that, I just… Christ, I can't get my head on straight."

Faith had noticed that. Normally, behavior like theirs would indicate anxiety and possibly guilt, but Faith didn't read them as guilty, only disoriented. Besides, Turk seemed to trust them, and she had learned to trust Turk's instincts.

At the moment, Turk had left Bonnie and was sidling up to Drew, looking up at him with the plaintive sympathy that only dogs could muster. Drew looked down, and like his wife earlier, calmed visibly at Turk's presence. He reached down and scratched Turk under the chin. "Good dog," he said, "My brother had a German Shepherd a while back. Taught it to hunt with him. He's got a Rottweiler now, good dog, but I think the Shepherd was better."

"Is there anything else you can tell us?" Faith said. "Anything at all, even if it doesn't seem important? Sometimes details that don't seem important at first turn out to be the critical pieces of evidence that help solve a case."

"Well," Drew said, "The only thing I can think of is that the fence used to be a flowerbed. When we moved in here, the Baxters' lot—that's the other side of where the fence will go—was still under construction. The border of our property was a large, wraparound flowerbed. I guess the previous owner liked open spaces. Anyway, we took the flowers out and put the fence up when we moved in, but the storm blew it down and now I have the Baxters nagging me to rebuild it."

"No one asked *you* to build it, Drew," Bonnie corrected. "You can hire a professional."

"The Baxters are your next-door neighbors?" Michael asked.

"Yes," Drew said. He frowned. "Didn't I say that?"

"Has anyone talked to them?" Faith asked.

Drew shrugged. "They were inside when I found the body. They might have come out to look with all the other looky-loos, but I didn't see them. Not that it means anything. I haven't been thinking straight. I coulda missed something."

Faith stood and handed him a card. "Well, if you think of anything, please give us a call right away."

"I will," he said.

Michael stood and said, "Sir, Ma'am, thank you for talking to us. Get some rest. Take tomorrow off if you can. Let us handle all the heavy lifting."

"Okay," Drew said. "Can I build the fence yet or do you guys need to keep digging around?"

Michael and Faith exchanged a look. "Let's hold off on the fence for now," Faith said. "When we're finished, we'll be happy to install a fence for you."

Michael lifted an eyebrow but didn't say anything as Bonnie said, "Oh, that would be wonderful. Thank you."

Faith called Turk and after allowing Drew and Bonnie to hug him goodbye, he followed the two agents out of the home.

"Boss isn't going to be happy about you offering the Bureau's money to build a fence," Michael said.

"The Boss can stick it," Faith said with more vehemence than she intended. "He's the one who wanted to stick us on a local case. He can deal with the fallout."

Michael looked searchingly at her. "You okay, partner?"

"Right as rain," she said. "Never better."

She stepped ahead of him to avoid more probing questions, and this time, she decided to drive.

Michael got in the car and said, "All right, so what do we think?"

"Almost certainly local," Faith said. "We'll want to focus our attention there. The key is to find a connection between the two victims. If we find that, we'll almost certainly have our killer."

"Well," Michael said, "Let's hope Cantor is as good as he seems."

Faith nodded in agreement, but some of her earlier confidence had faded. Something about the brazenness of burying a body in a neighbor's backyard worried her. She would have suspected the Miltons or their next door neighbors, but their alibi was ironclad and besides, all of Faith's instincts told her they were innocent.

But someone was guilty, and whoever it was knew how to hide in plain sight.

Jethro Trammell had hidden in plain sight.

The day was warm, and Faith wasn't running the air conditioning, but she shivered anyway.

CHAPTER FIVE

They drove to the coroner's office. Not surprisingly, it was located some distance away from Cedar Hills. Faith thought it was interesting that communities like Cedar Hills seemed almost to abhor any sign of police or fire services. The nearest precinct station was fifteen minutes away. The nearest fire station was twenty minutes away. There was a boutique health center located adjacent to the neighborhood featuring such essential services as a chiropractor, herbalist, yoga studio, and acupuncturist, but the nearest hospital was nearly as far away as the fire station. It was as though the idea of admitting a need for those services was as abhorrent as the need itself.

The coroner's office was a full half-hour away in the heart of the city, a safe enough distance from Cedar Hills and the other wealthy suburbs for the residents to easily pretend it didn't exist. They spoke little on the drive over, both of them mulling over the scene and waiting to see if anything stuck. It was a process that typically worked well for them but yielded little results at this moment.

When they arrived, the desk sergeant—the only uniform in the office, waved them through. "Rabbi's in the back," he said. "With the DBs."

"The Rabbi?" Michael asked.

"Cantor," the desk sergeant replied. "We call him the Rabbi. You know, cause—"

"I get it," Michael replied drily. "Thank you."

As they headed for the autopsy room, Michael said under his breath, "If I hear another goddamn nickname, I'm going to shoot someone."

Faith smiled but didn't reply. She was thinking of the first victim, the one they hadn't seen yet. Oftentimes the first victim was the most important in a murder investigation, especially in the case of serial killers. Officially, this wasn't a serial killer yet. That would require a third victim, a victim Faith hoped they wouldn't find but suspected they would before long.

The first victim was where killers made mistakes. They had never killed anyone before, and they might make mistakes out of anxiety or inexperience. Often, cases were solved by working backwards until investigators found the oldest victim and followed leads exposed in earlier killings.

So when she entered the room and found two bodies—the vic from earlier and a man's body slightly bloated and more decomposed than the first, she felt a rush of hope.

Cantor—she refused to think of him as the Rabbi—smiled at her, blushing again. "Special Agent Bold," he said, "good to see you."

"Good to see you too, Cantor," Michael said drily.

"Oh yes," Cantor said, his flush deepening. "And you too, Special Agent… uh…"

"Prince," Michael reminded him.

"Right." Cantor's smile widened when he saw Turk. "Hey boy! How are you?"

Turk barked formally, and Cantor stood straight and mimicked a salute. Turk regarded him with the same tolerant irritation with which every former Marine would regard such behavior.

Cantor didn't seem to notice Turk's irritation and laughed, ruffling Turk's fur before turning back to the agents. "So," he said, "Let's talk dead bodies."

He put on a pair of latex gloves and lifted the sheet off of both victims. Faith stepped closer, and after a moment's hesitation, Michael followed, grimacing slightly.

"As you can see," Cantor said, gently lifting both victims' heads with a comfortable ease that indicated his experience at this job, "they both died of a massive blunt-force trauma to the head."

"You can say that again," Michael said with another grimace. "Christ."

"What's interesting is that there are no other wounds of any kind on the victims," Cantor said, "No defensive wounds and nothing under their fingernails or on their teeth."

"Come again?" Michael asked.

Cantor smiled and when he spoke again, it was with the air of a professor eagerly answering a question he hoped would be asked. "When a person fights for their life, it's common to see bits of skin or hair under their fingernails or in their teeth from scratching and biting at their killer. Also common is bruising of the arms and legs and abrasions on the knuckles. These victims—" he gently set down their heads and lifted their hands in turn to illustrate "—display no such injuries."

"So they didn't struggle," Michael said.

"They did not," Cantor confirmed.

"So this was someone they knew," Faith said, "Or at least an attack they weren't expecting."

"Since the attacks were from the front, I would go with the former," Michael said. "If it was a surprise attack, I would expect the wounds to come from behind."

"Any sign of sexual contact?" Faith asked. "Semen or epithelial cells that would indicate the killer was someone intimately involved with either victim?"

"Well," Cantor said, "no on that for our male victim, but there *is* sign of sexual contact for our female victim."

Faith raised an eyebrow at that. "Oh?"

"Oh yes," Cantor said. "Not long before death, maybe ten or twelve hours."

Michael stepped closer, his discomfort with the bodies forgotten. "Any sign that this was nonconsensual?"

"Well, there's no sign of a struggle," Cantor said. "But that doesn't necessarily mean it was consensual."

"Did you get a DNA sample?" Faith asked.

"Yes," Cantor replied. "I got a sample and sent it to CSI. If it belongs to anyone in the system, we'll know in a day or two."

"Do we have an ID?" Michael asked. "That might help us find Romeo faster."

"Ah, yes," Cantor said. "Evelyn Vance, forty-one."

EV.

"Does Evelyn have a husband?" Faith asked.

"She does," Cantor said. "Derek Vance. I was actually going to notify him when you two showed up."

"Don't," Faith said. "We'll talk to him ourselves."

"Works for me," Cantor said. "I've never been good at talking to families anyway."

"What about the first victim?" Michael asked. "Do we have an ID on him?"

"Ethan Somersall," Cantor said, stepping over to the male victim. "Forty-six, married with two kids. Partner at a law firm, Porter and Somersall. I don't know much about them, but you guys are the detectives. I'm sure you'll learn more information faster than I ever could."

"Have you notified his family?" Faith asked.

"Not yet," Cantor said. "Should I wait to do that too?"

"Yes," Faith said.

"Ah," Cantor said, lifting an eyebrow conspiratorially. "I get it. "You want to see how they react when they learn about the death. See if they act guilty."

Faith felt a flash of irritation but reminded herself that Cantor wasn't an actual law enforcement officer so he couldn't know how irritating it was for a civilian to act like an armchair investigator. "Anything else we should know about our victims?" she asked.

"Well," Cantor said, "I don't know if it matters, but Ethan here—" he tapped the male victim "—would have been dead in six months or less no matter what."

Faith and Michael both reacted in surprise and Cantor explained, "Yeah, he had an aneurysm which was one bad day away from bursting. It's funny," he said, "if our killer had only sat tight a while longer, fate would have done the job for him. Well, for Ethan, anyway."

"With people like this, it's never about death," Faith opined. "It's about power. It wouldn't be enough for our killer for natural causes to take the victims. The killer needed to be the one to do it. He needed to be the one to end their lives."

"Or she," Michael interjected.

Faith rolled his eyes, "Yes, or she." To Cantor, she said, "Anything else we should know?"

"Well," Cantor said, "The victims were buried within a few hours of death, so they had to have been killed close to where they were buried."

That supported Faith and Michael's belief that the killer was local.

"They were also killed within a few days of each other. Ethan's been buried for maybe a week, Evelyn for three days."

That wasn't good. It meant this killer was moving fast, and with no connection between the victims other than the fact that they lived in the same neighborhood, there was a strong risk that another body would show up within the next few days.

Faith and Michael shared a look before turning back to Cantor.

"We need addresses for both victims," Faith said. "I'd like to talk to the families today, if possible."

"You'll have to move fast," Cantor said. "Sun's gonna set in a couple of hours."

"We'll work late," Faith said. "I guarantee our killer isn't keeping a nine-to-five schedule."

"No," Cantor said, "probably not."

***

Faith wanted to interview Ethan's family—the Somersalls—first, but when she called Mrs. Somersall, she learned that she was working late and wouldn't be home for another two hours. So, they headed to Derek Vance's house first.

As soon as Derek opened the door and saw the three of them standing there, Faith knew two things. First, she knew that he realized immediately why they were there. She knew this because his eyes widened and he whispered, "Oh God," before slowly sinking to his knees and burying his face in his hands, weeping uncontrollably.

The second thing she knew was that Derek Vance was not the murderer. She knew this because as soon as Derek fell to his knees, Turk walked right up to him and laid his head on the man's shoulder. Turk's instincts with people were spot on so far, and even if Faith didn't trust her own first impression that Derek's grief was genuine, she had learned to trust Turk's intuition.

Derek's arms instinctively wrapped around the dog and held him closely, shoulders heaving as he sobbed. Faith looked at Michael and saw the pain in his eyes that mirrored her own. When she finally spoke, she said, "Mr. Vance, I am so sorry."

He didn't respond, and Faith didn't make him do so. She stood next to Michael and waited patiently while Turk offered Derek a strong shoulder to cry on.

After several minutes, Derek's tears subsided enough that he was able to stand. He wiped his sleeve across his face and said, "I'm sorry. I'm Derek Vance, but I guess you two know that already."

"Special Agent Faith Bold, FBI," Faith said. "This is Special Agent Michael Prince."

Considering the circumstances, Faith didn't offer her hand, and Derek didn't offer his. He did invite them inside, however, and even had the presence of mind to offer them coffee. Faith accepted a cup, not because she needed caffeine, but because she knew Derek needed something to do so he could talk to them and not collapse into tears again.

Everywhere in the house were signs of Evelyn. The pictures that decorated every wall were the traditional, homey keepsakes that no straight man on Earth ever thought of but every man allowed his wife to put up. Faith knew they would remain there until Derek died. The embroidered towels hanging in the kitchen, the attractive arrangement of the furniture, and the ornamental throw that sat perfectly over the center of the loveseat that Faith knew would never be used again save for late night sessions weeping and holding his wife's photo, all spoke of the presence of a woman who would never again meet her husband's eye.

"She used to love this coffee shop," Derek said, handing Faith a cup. "Whole Earth Roasters. They're one of those environmentally friendly shops. She always got this organic blend." He chuckled. "It costs twenty dollars a pound and tastes just like the three-dollar-a-pound canned stuff I get at the supermarket." He smiled and said, "Evie used to get so angry with me when I would say that. I used to make fun of it just to watch her get riled up. She was so beautiful when she was mad." His smile faded, "So she's the body they found earlier today on Oak Crest Drive?"

Faith shared a glance with Michael. "How did you hear about that?" she asked.

"It's all over the news," Derek said.

Faith frowned. She supposed it was impossible to keep something like this off the news, especially when it happened in a neighborhood like Cedar Hills, but it still frustrated her that now the killer surely knew they were after him and would be taking steps to cover his tracks.

She managed to wipe the frown from her face quickly and said, "Yes. I'm so sorry."

Derek nodded and sighed. Later, Faith knew there would be longer and more bitter tears, but right now, he was in a state of shock and unable to do much more than simply absorb the information.

"I hate to ask this, Mr. Vance," she said, "But you don't know of anyone who might want to hurt Evelyn, do you?"

Derek shook his head. "No, no, I don't. Everyone liked her. She was the popular one. High school cheerleading captain, valedictorian in college, employee of the month more often than not at the office before she was promoted, life of every party. People always used to ask me how on Earth I managed to convince her to marry me. I was always shy and awkward."

He smiled as he said this, and his chest puffed up with pride. He was a very attractive man now, fit and youthful in appearance, with just enough ruggedness in his strong jaw and the lines around his eyes to make him look mature and distinguished. She imagined he was one of those men who grew into his looks later in life and so always believed that he was the awkward, geeky dork who was lucky beyond belief to have won the favor of a beautiful woman.

"Was she in pain?" he asked. "Did she…"

His lip began to tremble, and Faith quickly answered, "No. No, it was instant. She didn't suffer. She didn't even know she was dying."

She wasn't sure if saying that would comfort him or hurt him more, but he sighed and said, "That's good. At least she didn't spend her last moments in pain."

"Mr. Vance, how did your wife seem to you recently?"

Derek frowned. "What do you mean?"

"Did she seem distracted?" Faith asked, "Nervous, irritable. Any behavioral changes at all?"

He shook his head. "No. No, actually the past year or so she seemed much happier than normal. She had a hard time with turning forty, you know, but the past year, she was in good spirits." He smiled, "I told her she looked young again."

Faith and Michael exchanged another glance. Faith would bet her badge that she knew the reason for Evelyn Vance's sudden happiness. "Did she have any friends she would see alone?" she asked.

"Well, sure," Derek said, "She had girlfriends. Why do you ask? You don't think one of them did it, do you?"

Depends on who the man she cheated on you with is, Faith thought. Out loud, she said, "We're just trying to get a sense of who she was. We'll have a better sense of where to look the more we know about Evelyn's life."

"Any male friends?" Michael asked.

Faith shot him a warning glance, but it was too late. Derek frowned. "Are you saying she was cheating on me?"

"I'm not saying anything," Michael backpedaled. "We just need to consider all possibilities."

"Well, the answer's no," Derek said, jaw jutting. "Evelyn was a good woman. She would never hurt me like that."

"You're right," Michael said, "I'm sorry for the implication. One last thing. You're not a suspect, Mr. Vance, but would you mind if we got a hair sample from you? Just to make some confirmations so you don't show up on a naughty list you shouldn't be on."

Derek stared a moment before nodding and allowing Michael to pull a strand of his hair with tweezers and put it into an evidence bag.

"Anyone new in her life?" Faith asked once the sample was collected. "Not a lover, obviously," she clarified with a glare at Michael, "But any recent arrivals?"

"No," Derek said, sighing and shaking his head. "But…"

Faith raised an eyebrow.

"Well," Derek said, "I guess I wouldn't know. I mean, I know her girlfriends, but I was never really involved in that part of her life. I thought… well, I never asked her to come to my poker games. I guess I just thought she wouldn't want me tagging along with her girls."

"Can you please write down the names of Evelyn's closest friends, especially anyone who lives in or near Cedar Hills?" Faith asked. "We want to interview as many people as possible."

"Sure," Derek said, "Sure. I'll do that."

He wrote down maybe a half-dozen names, then handed the list to Faith. "That's all I can think of. The ones who live here, anyway."

"Thank you, Mr. Vance," Faith said, standing. She handed Derek a card. "If you think of anything else, please call me."

"I will," Derek said. "Just promise me one thing." His brow darkened. "Find the asshole who did this to Evie. Find him and you put him in the ground."

"We'll find him, Mr. Vance," Faith said.

"Good," Derek said.

The light fell from his eyes then. He slumped heavily into his seat and stared ahead blankly. He still sat there when Faith, Michael, and Turk left. Faith closed the door behind her and the three agents left for the Somersall residence.

Faith felt her confidence wane further. Logic didn't seem to apply to this case so far. The Miltons had no idea about a body buried days earlier on their property, but their alibi checked out. Derek Vance had a motive for at least one of the victims, but he was utterly unaware of the existence of that motive.

She knew it was dangerous to believe that the killer was intelligent enough to hide behind other people's potential motives, but the other option—that there was no rhyme or reason to the killings at all—scared her even more.

Hopefully their next interview would clear things up. They headed to the Somersall residence, reaching it five minutes after leaving Vance's place.

Martha Somersall took the news better than Derek Vance did. Faith suspected that had a lot to do with the presence of her kids, five in total, who were quickly sequestered in another room to watch a movie while Martha spoke with the agents.

Once more, Turk went immediately to comfort Martha, and Faith dismissed any suspicion that she could be responsible somehow for the killings. Not that the five-foot-one, hundred-pound Martha was likely to be capable of murdering anyone as brutally as Evelyn and Ethan were murdered. The professional in her thought it was dangerous to base her hunches on a dog's intuition, but the decade of experience she had with the Bureau taught her to rely on her hunches even when they seemed unlikely, and her hunch was that Turk's instincts were on target.

"So he's gone?" Martha asked.

"I'm afraid so, ma'am," Michael said gently.

He was taking point on this interview. Faith would never admit this to him out loud, but he had a special kind of charm with women. They seemed to instinctively open up to him. Women were occasionally more guarded with Faith. Not always guarded, but never so open as they were with Michael.

"You know who did it?" Martha asked.

"Not yet," Michael said. "We were wondering if you might have an idea who might want to hurt him."

She chuckled bitterly. "You want a list?"

Michael and Faith exchanged a look.

"Ethan is—was a very successful lawyer. I'm sure you've run into enough lawyers in your job to know that you don't get to be a successful lawyer by being a saint."

She waited for Michael to say something, and when he chose not to comment, she continued, "I won't go so far as to say that anyone wanted him dead enough to try to kill him, but there will be some dry eyes at the funeral."

"Any help you can give us would be invaluable," Michael said.

Martha shrugged. "Might as well start with the firm. Porter and Somersall on Freedom Street. Porter was close with him, but the junior partners were all just waiting for one of them to go to grab the senior partner job. Didn't have to be Ethan. They would have been just as happy to see George Porter go."

Michael folded his hands on the kitchen table and said, "Ma'am, this is difficult to ask, but do you have reason to believe that anyone may have suspected your husband of unethical behavior?"

Martha barked a short laugh and said, "You know he was a lawyer, right?" She laughed again, and said, "I mean, not really. Not any more unethical than anyone else, and nothing illegal. He was a shark, but he was tame, as far as sharks go."

"What about neighbors?" Michael said, "Anyone in the area who might have had a grudge against him? Did he have any feuds with anyone in Cedar Hills?"

Martha offered another bitter chuckle. "People here don't feud, Special Agent. Not unless you count putting up more and more garish Christmas lights every year. This is a *nice* neighborhood."

Her lip curled as she said that, and Faith thought that unconscious look of contempt told them more than anything else they had learned today.

"One final question, Mrs. Somersall," Michael asked. "Did your husband happen to know an Evelyn Vance or Derek Vance?"

She shook her head. "No. Why?"

"That was the other victim. Evelyn Vance."

"Was he sleeping with her?" she asked.

Michael blinked at the frankness of the question. "We don't believe so," he said.

Martha nodded. "Well, it probably wasn't her husband, then."

Michael didn't have a response for that.

Michael wrapped up the interview, getting a list from Martha of all of the neighbors with whom Ethan was in regular contact along with the names of the partners at Ethan's law firm. The children were growing rapidly more curious as the interview progressed and when one of them—a girl of maybe eight or nine—asked in a trembling voice why Mommy was talking to the police officers, Faith decided it was time for them to leave.

Martha showed them to the door, and just before Faith and Michael left her, her façade cracked. "What do I tell the kids? How do I tell them their daddy won't be coming home anymore?"

Faith didn't have an answer to that, and she didn't offer one.

As they drove back to the city, Michael asked, "So, what do we know?"

“Well,” Faith said, “we can be reasonably sure the killer is a neighbor, someone both victims knew and trusted. I think we start interviewing the names both families gave us. The killer has to be someone who lives here and knows the neighborhood well.”

“I agree,” Michael said, “I’m not even going to bother with Ethan’s firm. There’s no connection between Ethan’s firm and Evelyn Vance. I’ll send the hair sample to CSI and see if they can confirm whether the DNA is a match to the semen found on Vance. With any luck, that should give us a real suspect.”

“Good idea,” Faith said. “We should focus on the community.”

“You think we’ll get him before he gets someone else?” Michael asked.

Faith didn’t answer. She supposed that was all the answer Michael needed.

CHAPTER SIX

He worked the trowel under the soil, carefully fishing under the roots of the pigweed. This plant was budding and, if left alone would flower and spread its seeds throughout the whole garden. If he allowed that to happen, then he would spend the rest of his life fighting an infestation that would never be contained.

He finished with the trowel and wrapped a strong, calloused hand around the stem just above the soil. He pulled firmly, yanking the weed—roots and all—from the soil. He checked to ensure he hadn't left any roots behind. When he confirmed that the removal was clean, he nodded in satisfaction and stood.

His garden was pristine once more. Manicured rows of bluebells, golden rod, phlox, and bees balm shone in brilliant yellows and blues and reds while a raised box in the center housed his pride and joy, a stand of harlequin blue flag irises, their deep indigo blooms rising head and shoulders above the rest. The flowers would bloom for perhaps a month longer before the plants shed their blooms for winter. He would carefully remove the summer annuals and store them in his greenhouse for the winter, replacing them with violas, snapdragons, and poinsettias.

His work done, he headed inside, tossing the weed into a compost bin on the way. He changed out of his gardening clothes and headed for the shower.

As the water cascaded over him, washing away the dirt and mud of the day's business, he thought of weeds and their persistence in spite of all efforts to contain them.

That one pigweed plant was barely an eyesore in a field of beauty but left alone a day or two longer, it would have overcome his entire garden and then some. That was the nature of weeds. It was easy enough to ignore them, easier still when one considered the work necessary to remove them, but you couldn't leave them alone; if you did, they would spread.

Beauty was fragile. Ugliness was persistent. Left alone, a garden would always succumb to weeds. It was only with the dedicated, disciplined intervention of a knowledgeable gardener that weeds could be prevented from choking the life out of everything in their path.

Cedar Hills was much like his garden. Beautiful. Full of beautiful people in beautiful houses who led beautiful lives, good lives, the lives promised to them by a dream shared by the settlers of this great nation for the past four hundred years.

But as with all gardens, there were weeds, and those weeds, left unchecked, would choke the life and beauty out of the entire neighborhood if no gardener intervened.

He was an excellent gardener. Over the years, he had pulled many weeds from this neighborhood, and as a result, Cedar Hills was still beautiful.

He couldn't stop now. It was frustrating that Vance and Somersall had been discovered, but it didn't mean he should stop. You didn't stop caring for your garden just because it was storming outside. The weeds weren't harmed by the storm; they were strengthened by it. He needed to be vigilant, now more than ever.

He thought of the next weed to be pulled. His lips turned downward as he recalled the rumors he'd heard at the hardware store the other day. He was shopping for topsoil to replace what the recent storm had washed away and the next counter over, he heard Gabe Brant and Kieran Forrest talking about her.

He didn't take them at their word. Some weeds mimicked harmless plants, and it was important to be sure that what you were pulling really was a weed before you pulled it. He checked thoroughly, and only now that he was certain of the weed's identity would he pull it.

But he would pull it. If he didn't, it would spread its seeds throughout the entire community and choke the life out of the garden he had tended for the past fifteen years.

He finished his shower and toweled off. His body was older. His skin was leathery and lined with wrinkles. His eyes, once a startling blue, had faded into softness. He was older now.

But still strong. Muscles still rippled under that leathery skin and though the blue in his eyes was faded, the mind behind them was as sharp as ever. His hands lacked the softness of youth, but they were sure and capable.

The storm had come. The storm would pass. The weeds would be pulled. He would remain. His garden would remain.

CHAPTER SEVEN

Faith woke before dawn and rolled out of bed. Her bed creaked as she stood, and she heard the clicking of paws on tile as Turk woke and trotted immediately to her bedroom.

"Morning, boy," she said. "You ready to go catch some bad guys?"

Turk snorted half-heartedly, and Faith chuckled. "Yeah, you're probably right. This is going to be a long one."

She showered and dressed, and when she was done she called Michael. Michael answered with a reasonable degree of alertness and agreed to meet her at the office for coffee before heading to Cedar Hills to begin canvassing the neighborhood.

"Why the office?" he asked. "There are a dozen coffee shops on the way."

"Oh, get over it, you big grump," she said. "I'll bring some of that heirloom stuff and make you a special pot, all for wittle Michael."

"Screw you," he said. "But seriously, why the office?"

"I want to run some of the names we got through records," she said. "Actually, I want to run as many names through records as we possibly can. You're closer to the office than I am. Do you think you can get the names of all of the residents of Cedar Hills?"

"Jesus," Michael whined. "Really? You can't make an intern do that?"

"You can make an intern do that," Faith countered. "I'm going to bring you your precious craft coffee."

Michael grumbled a bit more but agreed to call ahead and have someone make the list. "So what, we're going to run them through NICBCS and see if anything pops up?"

"That's the plan," Faith said. "Bonus points for assault, burglary, domestic violence, all the usual hallmarks. You know, like ordinary detective work."

"If I wanted ordinary detective work, I would have joined the Police Department," Michael groused.

"Thank you, Prince!" Faith said cheerfully, hanging up before Michael could complain some more.

Her cheeriness vanished as soon as she hung up. The real reason she wanted to meet at the office was to make sure her files on the copycat killer case were still where she had left them.

She realized she was being paranoid. There was no reason on God's green Earth why anyone would feel a need to dig through her personal files, but she still worried. It wasn't a good sign. This kind of suspiciousness was a hallmark of guilt.

She knew this, but she couldn't stop herself. She needed to know that her case—and she still thought of it as her case—was safe.

She caught Turk staring at her and reddened. She was familiar enough with him now that many of his expressions were as recognizable to her as a human's and she could tell that he saw straight through the façade she put up for Michael.

God, she really was paranoid. She finished getting ready, grabbed the coffee from the pantry, and said, "All right, Turk. Let's go."

Turk kept his accusing stare on her as they drove to the office, and when they parked, Faith said, "I don't need your judgment too, okay? He hurt you like he hurt me. You should be on my side."

Turk didn't offer an opinion one way or another, but he looked away, so there was that, at least.

She met Michael at the break room, and said, "Hey, Prince. How's—"

He lifted his hand and pointed at the coffee. Faith rolled her eyes but couldn't suppress the smile that came to her face. "All right, you big baby," she said, "I'll make your precious coffee."

Ten minutes later, Michael took his first sip of the coffee. He closed his eyes and savored the brew a moment, then looked at Faith and said, "All right. I got the list printed. Vanessa is running it through records now. She said it could take a few hours, so unless you want to sit here and scratch your ass while we wait, I think we get a head start interviewing the friends and neighbors of the recently deceased."

"Works for me," Faith said. "Just give me a moment to check something."

"Check what?" Michael said, "Christ, you're more squirrelly than a groundhog in February."

"There is no way on Earth that's a saying," Faith said. "And you're from California."

"We have groundhogs in California," Michael said.

"Sure you do," Faith replied, grinning, as she walked out of the break room. Turk followed her, and she was grateful that Turk couldn't speak English, because he wore the same disapproving stare as earlier while she unlocked her file cabinet and confirmed that the files were exactly where she left them. She left immediately after confirming that, not wanting to get caught up in conversation. Fortunately, the boss had his back to her and Clark and Desrouleaux were nowhere in sight, probably already working on their investigative tasks for the day.

She reached Michael and the three of them headed to the car. On the way down, Michael looked searchingly at Faith. "You sure you're all right?" he asked.

"Fine," Faith said, forcing herself to make eye contact with him. "Never better."

***

Considering the mountainous task before them, Faith and Michael decided to split up. Michael would interview the list of names Martha Somersall had given, along with their close neighbors. Faith would do the same with Vance.

The interviews revealed little that they didn't already know, but the little that was revealed was telling. Evelyn Vance, it seemed, was not the saint her husband believed. Apparently, she was well-known around the community for playing the field, so to speak. Most agreed that Derek didn't deserve it, but a few of the more tenured neighbors opined that it wasn't surprising that a free-spirited, energetic woman like Evelyn wouldn't be satisfied with the meek, gentler Derek, movie-star looks notwithstanding.

Faith supposed she shouldn't be surprised to find that the people behind the manicured lawns and multiple luxury cars weren't as wholesome as they liked to appear, but it was still jarring, like biting into a donut to find it stuffed with mud and grime instead of cream.

The neighbors all told variations of the same story. Derek was meek and gentle and Evelyn was restless. According to some, she loved him but couldn't help herself. According to others, she never loved him and was a heartless bitch, but everyone agreed that she was unfaithful.

"You should talk to Derek," one particularly sour old man said. "Betcha anything he got fed up and did her in, himself."

Faith said she would take it under advisement, but she knew already that Derek wasn't the murderer. His reaction to the news of Evelyn's death was genuine and, besides, there was no connection between Evelyn and Ethan Somersall. None of the people Faith interviewed even knew who he was, except for a couple who saw an ad for his law firm on tv and asked if it was the same Somersall.

As far as suspects, the interviews proved that the neighbors were nosy and occasionally unpleasant, but most had ironclad alibis and the ones that didn't were very unlikely to be responsible for the murders. She took their contact information anyway and gave them the spiel about staying close by, but she didn't anticipate anything would come of it.

Faith's final interview was Barbara Eckersley, a matronly woman of about sixty who worked as a nurse-practitioner in the nearby medical center.

"That poor man," Barbara said. "He loved her so much. She meant the world to him, and she was so cruel to him."

Faith's ears perked up. "How so?" she asked.

"Well," Barbara said, waggling her hand. "I really shouldn't say."

She said this in a tone that made it clear to Faith that she was absolutely desperate to say it and hoped against hope that Faith would ask her to say it. Faith suppressed a wry smile and said, "Anything you know that can help us is appreciated, Ms. Eckersley."

"Well," Barbara said, "Between you and me—"

And everyone else you talk to, Faith thought.

"—Evelyn was quite the rolling stone. I just hope Derek never learns it. It would crush him to know that Evelyn ran around on him the way she did."

"Any idea who she might have been seeing?" Faith asked.

"Why?" Margaret said. Her eyes widened until they were big as dinner plates. "You don't think *he* did it, do you?"

"We're just looking for as much information as we can get right now, Ms. Eckersley," Faith said.

"Well, I don't know for *sure*, but I wouldn't be surprised if all the single men in Cedar Hills enjoyed a night or two with Ms. Evie. Probably some of the married men, too."

"Why don't you just go ahead and write their names down for me?" Faith asked, her heart sinking again. It was a longshot that any of Evelyn's lovers would simultaneously have a beef with Ethan Somersall, and the day was drawing to a close anyway. If Michael hadn't come up with anything and the records search didn't yield anything, she could work her way through Evelyn Vance's little black book tomorrow.

Barbara, of course, was all too happy to write down the names. Faith knew that when Barbara told this story to her book club while they drank far too much wine and spent absolutely no time discussing literature, she would make herself out to be the star of the show, the Miss Marple whose keen eye had broken open the case for the FBI. She would tell this story for the rest of her life, even if her "evidence" turned out—as Faith suspected—to be useless.

She couldn't wait to get out of that house, and while she didn't suspect Barbara of being the killer, she noted that Turk was far less affectionate with her than with the others they interacted with.

After leaving, she called Michael. "Prince," he said.

"Dammit," she quipped. "I was looking for the frog."

"Ha ha," he replied. "I take it you're finished for the day?"

"Thankfully, yes," she answered.

"Ah. So you also wasted your time?"

"Yep. Everyone loves gossip, but none of that gossip is useful. So you didn't find anything either?"

"Nothing useful. Half the neighbors admired Ethan and half despised him. Most of them didn't care either way, but none of them are the type to kill and none of them even knew who Evelyn Vance was."

"Same here," Faith said, "which is really frustrating, because we can't have a suspect until we meet someone who knows both of them."

"Well, let's not lose faith, Faith," Michael said. "Maybe NICBCS has found something."

"Really?" Faith said. "A pun?"

"That was at least as good as your prince and the frog reference," Michael countered.

"Fair enough," Faith conceded.

They met back at the office, and when they reached Michael's desk, they compared notes. Essentially, they had encountered the same things. Rumors, gossip, and suspicions, most of them probably true, but none of them helpful. Fortunately, ten minutes after they arrived, Michael's desk phone buzzed.

"Prince," he said.

He listened for a moment, then smiled at Faith and said, "Yes, please. Thank you, Vanessa."

He hung up and said, "NICBCS popped on some of our neighbors."

Faith's eyes widened in anticipation. Now they were getting somewhere. "Let's see it," she said.

Michael opened the folder Vanessa emailed to him and they scrolled through. Faith's eyes widened further, and her mouth dropped open as well after a moment.

"God," Michael said, reading through the list, "you think you know a neighborhood."

The report was literally filled with noise complaints, domestic disturbances, accusations of theft, vandalism, abuse, drug possession, violence, and threats of violence. If Faith didn't know to which neighborhood the report referred, she would have assumed a low-income urban high-rise, not the pristine near-wealthy Cedar Hills.

"Hold on," Michael said. "Look at these."

He pointed to a heading labeled Missing Persons. Faith opened it, and her eyes widened. There were only nine disappearances over the past fifteen years, not an excessively high number, but what caught her eye was that the disappearances had increased dramatically in the past five years. Five of the missing persons had died in the past three years; again, not quite high enough to raise alarms, unless you happened to be investigating two murders in the past ten days.

The killer was escalating. Unfortunately, knowing that people were missing didn't help them without further investigation.

"Well," Faith said, "this doesn't really help us in the short term. It might help us find a connection or it might just complicate things further."

"Nope," Michael said. "Unless they all have a group murdering session every few days, this doesn't really narrow things—hold on."

He stopped scrolling and double-clicked on one of the names—Marcus Washington. Faith leaned over him to read and whistled when she saw the file. The picture was a mugshot—that was the first indicator that there was more than just petty neighborhood disputes on his rap sheet.

Much more.

CHAPTER EIGHT

Marcus Washington was a convicted felon who spent fifteen years in the state penitentiary for second-degree murder. The mugshot was from his arrest. Apparently, he and a fellow ne'er-do-well had gotten into a dispute at a bar and Marcus split his skull open with a beer bottle. Prior to his murder conviction, he had a long history of violence—assault, armed robbery, and harassment. At the time of his arrest, he had no fewer than three active restraining orders.

His rap sheet showed nothing after his release three years ago, but that didn't necessarily mean he was clean, just that he was better at hiding the dirt. As Faith skimmed the file, she said, "Well, I guess we're taking our evening coffee to go."

"Yes," Michael said, "looks that way. Did you see where he lives?"

"Cedar Hills, right?" Faith asked.

"Yes, but not just Cedar Hills."

He pointed at the map that showed his residence and Faith saw it was nearly halfway between the Somersall and Vance residences.

"Well, what do you know," Faith said.

"Let's go pay Mr. Washington a visit," Michael said.

"Let's," Faith agreed.

On the way back to Cedar Hills, Faith wondered aloud, "How does a convicted felon with no work history manage to buy a million-plus dollar home in a wealthy neighborhood?"

"Beats me," Michael said. "Maybe he has friends in low places."

"Maybe he held the owner at gunpoint and bought it for pennies then buried the bodies under three feet of dirt," Faith said.

Michael glanced at her. "I can't tell if you're joking or not."

"Me either," Faith said.

By the time they reached the house, dusk had long since given way to night. Faith was worried they might be too late and be forced to wake Washington up, but there was a light on in the living room when they parked. She resisted an urge to draw her weapon but kept a hand near her shoulder holster as they approached the house.

Turk stayed in front of her, ears perked and tail switching back and forth. Faith appreciated having him near. The last time she had confronted a violent criminal, she would have died if not for Turk's presence.

Faith stepped to the door and knocked with the hand not hovering over her weapon. Turk tensed and Michael lifted his own hand to his shoulder.

The door opened and Marcus answered. He was nearly twenty years older than he was in his mugshot, and those years showed. The bull-necked, powerful man of the mugshot was now a stooped, elderly man whose muscle had given way to flab. He regarded the agents with mild suspicion.

"Good evening," he said softly. "Can I help you?"

His hands were clearly visible, but Faith kept her hand close to her weapon in case he was hiding something. "Marcus Washington?" she asked.

"Yes, this is he," Marcus replied. "May I ask who you are?"

"Special Agent Faith Bold, FBI," she said. "This is my partner Special Agent Michael Prince and my K9 unit, Turk."

Marcus nodded. "May I see some identification, please?"

His tone was mild and his posture relaxed. Faith wasn't sure if this was because he had nothing to hide or because he was confident he had hidden it well. She produced her ID, and after a quick examination, he nodded and handed it back. "May I ask what this is about, Special Agent?" he asked.

"We're investigating the murders of Evelyn Vance and Ethan Somersall," Faith replied. "We'd like to ask you some questions."

She watched his reaction closely as she spoke. His eyes betrayed no surprise at the question but betrayed no guilt either. He nodded and sighed. "Well," he said, "I suppose I figured you guys would want to talk to me sooner or later. Would you like to come inside?"

"Yes, thank you," Faith said.

Marcus opened the door and led the three of them into the house. Turk seemed far less tense to Faith, and although he remained wary of Marcus, his eyes had lost that glint that came when he anticipated violence.

The house was modestly decorated, but well-appointed. The furniture was designed for comfort, with a massaging armchair and a thickly upholstered sofa. The carpet was plush and seemed newly installed. Faith nearly removed her shoes before stepping on it, but Marcus noticed and waved for her not to bother.

"I have cleaners come once a month," he said, "Twice a year they clean the carpet for me too, so don't worry about stains."

Indeed, the entire place seemed spotless. The walls gleamed white and the wood of the massive entertainment system that housed a sixty-five-inch smart tv was polished to a high shine.

Marcus motioned for them to sit. "You folks want something to drink?" he asked. "Coffee, water? I'm guessing you can't drink beer while you're on duty."

He smiled when he said that, and Faith could detect no hint of animosity. "We're fine, but thank you," she said.

Marcus nodded acknowledgment and sat in his easy chair, grimacing with effort.

"Nice place you got here," Michael mentioned.

Marcus smiled when Michael said that. "You're wondering how does an old felon like me afford a nice place like this."

"The thought had crossed my mind," Michael said.

"Well, I am blessed to have a family that still loves me in spite of the mistakes I've made in my life," Marcus said. "Among that family is a mother who never once lost faith that her little boy would learn the error of his ways and live a life glorifying to God. I don't know much about God; and if He is out there somewhere judging the sins of man, I doubt that He'll have much of an inclination to grant me a spot in Heaven after what I done, but Ma never stopped loving me."

His smile faded as he spoke, and Faith saw real pain in his eyes. Turk walked up to him and as he'd done with so many others during the investigation, he rested his head on Marcus's lap and allowed the older man to stroke his fur.

Marcus's smile returned. "You have a good dog," he said to Faith. "Anyway, Ma left me the house when she died, and enough of my Pa's money to let me live in comfort and peace for the rest of my life, which is exactly what I intend to do."

"So you don't work?" Michael asked.

"I volunteer mostly," Marcus said. "Weekends at the soup kitchen, weekdays at the Y. Sometimes I help out the younger folk cleaning up the streets when my arthritis isn't too bad."

Michael and Faith shared a look. Marcus was looking less and less like a killer with every passing moment.

Still, appearances could be deceiving and plenty of serial killers seemed saintly on the outside. John Wayne Gacy volunteered at a children's hospital, and he had killed over thirty people. Turk seemed to think Marcus wasn't a threat, but while Faith trusted his instincts, she wasn't yet ready to rule Marcus out as a suspect.

"You mentioned you knew we were coming to talk to you," Faith said. "Why is that?"

Marcus chuckled. "This is a nice neighborhood, Special Agent Bold. I doubt you'll find many other convicted criminals in Cedar Hills."

You'd be surprised, Faith thought. Out loud, she said, "So you believed that your criminal past would cause us to suspect you of these murders?"

"Well, it did, didn't it?" Marcus replied, his smile a little sad. "No need to beat around the bush, Special Agent. If I was you, I'd think the same thing."

"Well, the more honest you are with us, the faster we can rule you out as a suspect," Faith said. Or convict him, but she didn't feel a need to mention that.

"All right," Marcus said, "Well, I didn't kill them, but I'm guessing you can't just take my word for it."

Faith didn't respond directly to that. "Did you know either of the victims, Mr. Washington?"

"I knew Ethan Somersall by sight," Marcus said, "Not much more than that. When I moved in here, he offered his services to me. Claimed he could get my record expunged if I paid him five hundred dollars an hour for a year or two. I thanked him but told him I'd rather not have my record expunged. 'I'm a criminal,' I told him. 'I'm a reformed criminal, but I want to remember, not forget.'" He laughed. "Boy, you should have seen his face when I said that. He looked like someone just told him the sun was made of pork rinds."

"May I ask why?" Faith asked. "Why you want to keep your criminal record."

Marcus sighed and his smile faded as he stared into the distance. "Prison is a hellish place, Special Agent Bold. I guess you know that. It's a hellish place, but I guess I needed to go to hell for a while. I learned a lot in prison. I learned that I'm not as hard as I thought I was. I'm not the kind of person who can live a life hurting others."

"What brought you to that revelation?" Michael asked, a touch of sarcasm in his voice.

Marcus turned heavy eyes to Michael and said, "Prison gives you time to think, Special Agent. That's one thing people always say that's true. It gives you time to think. Every day, I thought of the man I killed.

I thought of the way his head split open when I cracked him with that beer bottle. I thought of the shock I felt when he didn't get up and I knew I'd killed him. I thought of the tears in my mother's eyes when the judge read the verdict. Mostly, I thought of myself, and how I never did grow up to be an astronaut or a fireman or a doctor or the President or any of the things I thought I would be when I was a child."

"I grew up to be a murderer, Special Agent."

He let the words hang a moment, and Faith could see the pain in his eyes like a tangible thing, something she could reach out and touch if she wanted. She knew for sure then that he wasn't their killer. Years of interacting with killers had sharpened her senses, and she could tell that Marcus was telling them the absolute truth right now. She would finish interviewing him because hunches never substituted for good detective work, but she knew that she would only confirm that he wasn't their guy.

After a pause, Marcus continued. "I grew up to be a murderer, and all I can do now is leave that life behind and maybe do some good in the world before I go. I can't make up for what I did. I never will. But I can do a little for as long as I can, and I can live peacefully with all men until I reach my own end."

He fell silent again, and when Faith was confident he was finished, she asked, "Did you have any contact with Mr. Somersall after you rejected his offer of representation?"

"No," Marcus said. "No, that was it. I never met Evelyn Vance either. I know that's your next question."

"Can you tell me your whereabouts this past Friday?" Faith asked.

"Sure can," he said. "I was at the Y from eight a.m. until four p.m., then I headed straight here. The Y can confirm my presence there. I'm afraid I can't provide any proof that I was in my home after that. Maybe you can check my phone? I hear you can track phones now."

"We'll keep that in mind," Faith said. "Can I assume you were at the Y Monday through Friday and the soup kitchen both of the past two weekends?"

"Sure was," Marcus said, "Home after that, so like I said, I don't really know how to prove that."

"We'll look into it," Faith said, deciding there was nothing more to be gained by talking to him.

She got the number for the soup kitchen where Marcus volunteered his weekends. She would confirm his day shifts with the Y and the soup kitchen and check his utility usage for the evenings to see if there were any dips in usage that could suggest he was out late at night. She knew already that he was innocent, though. He of all the people she had interviewed seemed ironically the least likely to be responsible for the murders.

They left once they got the numbers and elicited a perfunctory promise from Marcus to stay in town and call them if he thought of anything helpful. On the way back to the office to drop Michael off at his car, they discussed the interview.

"So I'm thinking he's not the guy," Michael opined.

"No," Faith said, "definitely not."

Turk barked in agreement and Faith offered a half smile that disappeared almost immediately. "I'll check the alibi just to be sure," she said, "but I think he might be one of the lucky ones who actually left crime behind when he left prison."

"Yeah," Michael said. He was silent a moment, then added, "Is it cynical of me to think that maybe if his rich mother hadn't left him a ton of money, he might not have been so motivated to give up crime?"

Faith shrugged. "It's no more cynical than believing that most crime comes from people who have nothing and see no other option."

"No," Michael said, "I guess not."

They finished the rest of the drive in silence. Faith glanced at Turk and saw him staring forlornly out at the passing lights. Faith reached behind and scratched him behind the ears, then left her hand there as she too stared out into the night.

CHAPTER NINE

Ariana smiled as she looked around her kitchen and envisioned the new granite countertops and stainless-steel smart appliances she would soon have. Her grandfather had *finally* kicked the bucket and had left her the lion's share of his inheritance. Granted, it was far less money than she was hoping for but it would be enough to redo her kitchen. She'd had to place her grandma in a far less expensive home than she planned originally, but there wasn't anything she could do about that. It wasn't like she was going to move an incontinent eighty-nine-year-old woman in with her and Dom.

She grinned at that thought. With Grandma safely ensconced in a home and Dom out of town until tomorrow, she had the house all to herself.

Well, hopefully not completely to herself. She giggled as she thought of the lacy red panties and bra she wore underneath her short skirt and low-cut halter top. If everything went well, she would soon be wearing them for Hector, and if everything went *really* well, she wouldn't be wearing them for long.

There was a knock on the door, and Ariana jumped, startled. She caught sight of her reflection in the kitchen window and laughed at herself. God, she was jumpy as a mouse.

There was another knock and she called playfully, "Ay, Hector, give me a second! You'll get to play, don't worry."

She sauntered to the door, letting her hips sway even though Hector wasn't yet inside to see it. She stopped a second to tease her hair and smooth her skirt, then opened the door.

It wasn't Hector. It was… she wasn't sure who it is. He looked familiar. Maybe a neighbor or one of Dom's coworkers from the Christmas party last year?

"Hello," she said, "can I help you?"

The man removed his hat—an old fedora like the ones they wore in old detective movies—and held it in front of him. The action revealed a head of gray hair and a closer look revealed lines in his face and hands. He was in good shape for his age, but he was probably closer to sixty than fifty.

Ariana relaxed a little and realized that she had been nervous at first. She nearly laughed at herself again but managed to stifle it.

The man smiled at her and asked in a soft voice, "Good evening, ma'am. Are you Ariana Gonzalez?"

"Yeah, that's me," she said. "Why? I'm sorry, do I know you?"

The stranger ignored her question and instead of answering, asked one of his own. "Have you recently come into a large sum of money?"

A quiet alarm went off in Ariana's head. "That's none of your business," she said stiffly.

"Oh, but it is," the man said, his voice still soft and gentle. "It very much is my business."

A much louder alarm went off in Ariana's head. "I'm calling the police," she said.

Her voice sounded shrill in her ears. She hated that, but she didn't have to dwell on it for long because when she tried to close the door, he blocked it with his foot and shoved it open.

Ariana stumbled backward with a cry, and her first thought as the stranger walked into her house was, *Oh my God, he's so strong.*

The stranger wasn't smiling anymore. His eyes, as soft and gentle as his voice a moment ago, were hard as diamonds now. He lowered the hat, and Ariana saw a thick leather baton in his other hand.

Ariana recognized the tool from one of those weapons shows Dom liked watching on tv, the one where geeks compared different fighters from history and tried to decide who would win in a battle.

It was a sap. She recalled thinking it was a silly name for a weapon, like the goop that fell off a tree.

It didn't seem so silly anymore.

The man raised the sap over his head. Ariana drew in breath to call for help, but before she could scream, stars exploded in her vision. The last thing she knew before consciousness left her was the dull thump of her body hitting the floor.

CHAPTER TEN

Faith sighed as she got into the passenger seat next to Michael. Another day, another dollar, the saying went. She was pretty sure no one had yet coined the phrase another day, another pointless waste of time interviewing men who were clearly not above sleeping with their married neighbor but just as clearly not the one responsible for her murder.

Michael had endured a similarly fruitless day. The partners at Porter and Somersall were—as promised, not at all displeased by the sudden vacancy of a senior partner position, but all of them had ironclad alibis that proved they hadn't been to Cedar Hills since the Fourth of July party they attended to suck up to their then boss. He had even interviewed some of the relatives of the older missing persons and found nothing helpful. No connection to each other, and no indication that the relatives were responsible for any of the disappearances.

Michael spoke first. "Well, phooey."

"I could think of a different word," Faith said.

Michael chuckled mirthlessly. "So could I," he said.

"So what do you want to do?" Faith asked.

"I'll tell you what I don't want to do," Michael said. "I don't want to drive back to the city to get three hours of sleep before waking up to do it all over again."

"You want me to drive?" Faith asked.

"I was thinking we just stay here," he said. "There's a relatively inexpensive hotel ten minutes away."

"You're going to pay for a hotel room to save twenty minutes of driving?"

"Forty minutes," Michael said. "You have to count both ways. And I'm not going to pay for the room; the Bureau is."

"I'm sure the Boss will be overjoyed at that," Faith said drily.

"The Boss put us on a PD case as a favor to his buddy the DA," Michael said. "He can stick his budget up his ass."

"I'm not so sure he'll see it the same way," Faith said.

"I'm pretty damn sure I don't give a rat's ass," Michael said.

Faith raised an eyebrow and Michael sighed. "Sorry. I just…" He lifted his hand and let it drop.

"Yeah," Faith said, "I get it."

Michael chuckled. "You'd think after fifteen years I'd get used to this. I mean, it's not like this is the first time a case involved days and weeks and even months of tedium before finding anything useful. Still bugs the hell out of me every time."

"Yeah," Faith agreed. "Me too."

"So what do you say?" Michael asked. "Hotel tonight? I won't tell David if you don't tell Ellie."

Faith offered a half-hearted smile at the joke. "Fine," she said. "But not yet. I'm going to walk Turk."

Michael raised his eyebrow. "Walk Turk? You've been walking him all day!"

"I'm going to walk him again," she said. "Clear my head a little in the process. Maybe something will settle into place."

Michael nodded. That had been known to work for Faith before. "All right. So you want me to wait here or pick you up?"

"It's up to you," Faith said, opening the door. "I might be a little while."

"Well, pizza's on you, then," Michael said.

"Deal," Faith replied, calling for Turk to follow her.

She started off down one of the winding paths that led through the various patches of grass and trees that lay scattered throughout the community. After a quarter-mile or so, she came across two uniforms patrolling the neighborhood. They lifted their hands as she and Turk passed by but offered no other form of acknowledgment.

She passed two other patrols over the next mile before turning down a path that led through the broad central park of the community. The park was well-lit, and in the distance, Faith could make out two other pairs of patrolling officers, but she was grateful for Turk's presence, nonetheless.

The path was brightly lit as well. Perfectly lit, in fact. The lampposts spaced every twenty yards or so cast enough light that the entire park was visible, but the light was mild enough that it still allowed for an impression of walking through an enchanted forest or perhaps a romantic forest depending on one's mood and choice of companion.

This was a nice neighborhood.

Faith had lost count of how many times she'd had that thought or the one that followed. This didn't seem like the kind of place where people were murdered and then buried in backyards.

But it was, and every day spent here chipped away at the pristine façade Cedar Hills tried so hard to present, revealing the dirty secrets underneath. Everyone had a skeleton or two in their closet. People were never so perfect as they seemed. Cedar Hills was really no different than anywhere else in that regard.

"But it's *supposed* to be different," she said aloud.

She stopped, playing that thought over in her mind. Cedar Hills was supposed to be different.

That seemed important, but Faith wasn't sure why. She repeated it to herself but got nothing more than an inquisitive stare from Turk.

She sighed and smiled down at him. "Maybe I'm just going crazy."

Turk snorted at that, and Faith's eyes narrowed. "I'm going to assume you meant to say, 'Of course not, Faith, you're just as sane as ever.'"

Turk tossed his head as if to say, "Whatever you want to believe."

Faith chuckled and said, "All right, boy. Let's head back to the car before Michael decides to leave without us."

As they walked back to the car, Faith looked around at the perfectly trimmed lawns, the exquisitely dimmed lights, and the multistory homes, and repeated once more, "It's supposed to be different here."

Once more, the phrase refused to offer her any insight, so she put it in the back of her mind and thought about dinner.

When she reached the car, she said, "I was thinking. How do you feel about Chinese takeout instead of pizza?"

Michael glared at her. "I think we're going to eat whatever the hell I feel like after waiting here for over an hour for you."

"There's a nice hole-in-the-wall in Pine Grove," Faith said, ignoring his grousing as she strapped herself in.

Michael sighed. "Fortunately for you, the hotel is located in Pine Grove."

He started the engine and backed out of the space, then accelerated away from Cedar Hills. "You're still buying," he said to Faith.

"Yep," she said. "I heard you the first time."

***

Faith struggled briefly against the straps tying her to the chair, but they didn't budge. She looked around for something, anything she could use to free herself. She found a tray a few yards away on top of which sat a rusty wood saw and an equally rusty bowie knife. A chill ran through her as she thought of what those tools were intended to do.

She took a breath to steady herself. If she could reach the tools before Trammell returned—

Too late.

The door opened and a sliver of white-hot light seared Faith's vision. She squinted and blinked until the door closed and the only light was once more the soft glow that filtered in through the barn's single high window.

Trammell approached and said in his tremulous voice, "Well, hello there, little lady. I sure am tickled to see you."

He walked to the tray and picked up the knife, running a finger lovingly across the blade. "The last one cried when she died, Faith. Will you cry?"

She wouldn't scream. She wouldn't give him that satisfaction. He could hurt her. He could kill her if he wanted, but she wouldn't scream.

Trammell walked closer, leaning forward until her nostrils flared from his sour breath as it wafted over her. "It's supposed to be different here," he said.

Faith frowned. That wasn't right. That's not what he said. He said, "Let's see how you bleed, little girl." He didn't say, "It's supposed to be different here."

She fixated on that sentence. If she could just understand what it meant, she could stop this. She could stop this before—

But then Trammell's knife sliced through the tendons behind her knee and Faith screamed after all.

Faith woke with a gasp. A thick, wet thing slid over her face, and she pushed it away instinctively. Her hands connected with something furry, and that was when reality snapped back into place.

She was in the hotel room. Michael was snoring on the other bed. The table was littered with empty takeout boxes and the tv played a thirty-minute commercial about coins at low volume.

She sighed and rolled over, placing her feet on the floor. "Sorry, boy," she said, "I didn't know it was you.

Turk sidled next to her and whined.

"Yeah, yeah, I know," she said. "I need to go see someone about this."

Turk whined again, and Faith thought she could hear an accusation in his voice. She stood and kept her eyes averted as she pulled on her sweatpants and t-shirt then stepped outside to get a candy bar from the vending machine, but mostly to give herself a moment away from Turk's plaintive stare.

She had no luck with that, because as soon as the door opened, Turk followed her outside. Faith sighed and decided to allow him to come.

"I don't think they have dog treats," Faith said. "But if they have those crème cookies you like, I'll buy you a pack."

They did have the crème cookies Turk liked, so Faith bought a pack for him and a chocolate bar with caramel and peanuts for herself. She wasn't much for chocolate—she was probably the only person she knew who wasn't—but it gave her something to focus on other than the thoughts that plagued her.

The nightmares weren't getting worse, but they weren't getting any better. Since she'd learned of the copycat Donkey Killer, it seemed that even when she was preoccupied with something else—a hot veterinarian, an important case—a part of her mind was fixated on the copycat.

A quieter but more assertive voice told her that a part of her was still in Trammell's barn, tied to a chair and screaming as her tendons were severed.

A twinge of pain behind Faith's knee caused her to grimace. It had been weeks since her injuries had flared up. Maybe the nightmares affected her body as well as her mind.

Turk finished the cookies and looked expectantly back at the vending machine. Faith smiled and shook her head. "No more for you. I want Dr. David to be happy with us at your next checkup."

Turk whined and cast a final glance at the vending machine before following Faith back to the hotel room. Faith tossed the wrappers in the combination ashtray/trash can near the room and headed back inside.

Michael rolled over when the door opened, his hand reaching under his pillow. He stopped when he saw Faith and grumbled as he turned over again. "Next time, you're getting your own room," he groused.

"Oh, say it ain't so," Faith said drily. "I'll be good from now on. Honest."

Without looking, Michael tossed a pillow at her over his shoulder. She caught it and tossed it back at him. It landed over his head, and he left it there.

Faith chuckled and got into bed. Turk jumped immediately into bed next to her. She let him stay there, and this time when she closed her eyes, the nightmares didn't return.

CHAPTER ELEVEN

Faith took another sip of her coffee while Michael talked with Sheriff Morton. It was an hour past dawn, and already at least a dozen K9 units were scouring the neighborhood for signs of any more bodies. For the moment, the residents tolerated the police presence. She wondered how long it would take for them to forget their fear of a killer and decide that the police presence was more of an annoyance than a help.

Turk whined next to her and looked ahead, his tail switching back and forth. Faith smiled. "You want to go help them, boy?"

Overhearing her, the sheriff turned and said, "If you want to help, I wouldn't mind another set of eyes."

Faith shook her head. "I think you guys have that covered. I want to look into our victims more. Did you get those phone records yet?"

Morton nodded. "Should be in your inbox," he said.

"Good," Faith said. "In that case, we'll go back to the hotel and see if we can find anything useful."

Morton lifted an eyebrow. "You guys are staying in a hotel? Don't you live in the city?"

"We wanted to be right on top of the action," Michael answered.

Faith suppressed a wry smile. This had nothing to do with being on top of the action and everything to do with Michael running up the bill for the Boss. Her partner was an excellent agent, but a very petty one at times.

Morton shrugged, and Michael said, "Faith, I really don't want to be cooped up in the room all day. I think we should go interview some more neighbors."

Faith couldn't imagine a greater waste of time considering the lack of progress they'd made so far on that front, but she decided to meet Michael halfway. Besides, she could use a few hours to herself.

"Take Turk and help the K9 units," she said. "I'll go to the hotel myself and see if I can find anything in the phone records."

"I can't take Turk," Michael said, "You're his handler. If the Boss finds out that you sent me to work with him, it'll be my ass."

“As soon as he learns you’re putting two hundred dollars a night on the Bureau’s credit card for a hotel room we don’t need it’s your ass,” Faith countered. “Look, you’re restless, Turk is restless, and I’m not restless, so why don’t the two restless special agents work out some of their energy while the only special agent who isn’t restless takes some time to think in peace and quiet.”

Michael sighed and said, “All right, Turk. Guess your mom needs some me-time. Sheriff, where do you want us?”

Morton, who had observed this exchange with the wooden impassivity of a thirty-year veteran of law enforcement, handed Michael a map and began to point out the areas he wanted them to canvass. Faith waved goodbye to Turk, who looked excited for a chance to stretch his legs, and headed back to the car. Faith began digging through Ethan’s phone records as soon as she reached the hotel.

Six months’ worth of phone records was a massive pile of information to dig through. As with most of the information they’d gathered since taking the case, it was almost entirely useless. There were the typical exchanges between husband and wife, mostly Honey-could-yous and shopping lists. Most of these were texts.

The exchanges with his partner and employees were mostly phone calls, interestingly enough. They probably thought that was more confidential than texts. They paid a service to expunge their records, but that only worked for local police forces, not the FBI. Morton had no doubt called the field office to get them to process the request through the FBI and not the Sheriff’s Department. It was a smart move, and she liked him more for it.

The phone calls revealed nothing illegal or even suspicious. They confirmed Martha’s assertion that Ethan was just as sleazy as every other successful lawyer in most respects, but like every other successful lawyer, he was very good at avoiding any form of sleaziness that could lead to prosecution. He was a jerk to his underlings, but not so much that it might inspire them to kill him, and nowhere was Evelyn or Derek Vance mentioned.

It took Faith a solid three hours to dig through Ethan’s phone records and find absolutely nothing useful. She sighed and started on Evelyn’s.

That yielded something almost immediately.

Evelyn Vance was cheating on her husband, but she wasn’t sleeping with any willing guy who looked twice at her. She was sleeping with only one other man, and that man—one Beau Carpenter—seemed very unhappy with Evelyn's decision to stay with her husband rather than leave. His requests started as half-serious jokes, then progressed to pleading that grew ever more impassioned. Right around the time that pleading turned to accusations and name-calling, Evelyn had decided to break off contact, about a week before she was murdered.

Then, of course, he had called her and apologized, and of course, she had eventually relented and taken him back. That was the night before her death.

Bingo.

Or was it? If Evelyn was the only body, Faith would have thought they had their man, but what did this have to do with Ethan? Beau showed up nowhere in Ethan's texts and a quick search through the files Vanessa had dug up on the neighborhood showed that Beau lived on the other side of the community, farther away from Ethan than Evelyn was.

Faith tapped her fingers on the table. She felt like the answer was there in plain sight, but she just couldn't grasp what it was.

"It's supposed to be different," she whispered.

Why did that phrase stick in her mind? What did it mean? *What* was supposed to be different?

She was startled away from her thoughts when her phone rang. She jumped and sighed in exasperation when she saw the call was from Michael.

"Bold here," she said, "You'll be happy to know that you scared the shit out of me. Hey, while I have you on the phone, guess what I found?"

When Michael spoke, his voice was taut with urgency. "Faith, you need to meet me at Marcus Washington's house. There's an honest-to-God mob outside."

Faith's blood chilled. "On my way. Is PD on scene?"

"A few," Michael said. "More are coming."

"Are you and Turk safe?" she asked, pulling on her shoes.

"We're fine," Michael said, "but if the crowd gets their way, Marcus won't be for long."

"Jesus," Faith said. "I'll be there in ten minutes."

She hung up and rushed from the room, grabbing her shoulder holster and jacket and putting both on as she sprinted to the car.

When Faith arrived at the scene, she saw with alarm that Michael wasn't exaggerating by calling it an honest-to-God mob. There were dozens of people crowded in front of Marcus's house and over a dozen officers struggling to maintain order.

Faith parked fifty yards from the house and approached from the side, cutting across several lawns to avoid pushing through the crowd. As she got closer, she could hear people shout, "Killer!" "Murderer!" "Get out!" and various other less polite phrases.

Michael was standing with Turk just behind the wall of police officers. Turk was growling and baring his teeth, and when he saw Faith, he immediately shot to her side. Faith reached down and patted his head to calm him, then asked Michael, "What's going on?"

"What does it look like?" he said testily. "Turk and I were snooping around the hills behind the house when Turk suddenly stopped like he smelled something. Next thing I know, he shoots off like a bullet and leads me here where I find these assholes—" he pointed at three men at the front of the growing crowd "—beating on Marcus's doors and telling him to come out or they were going to come get him. Fortunately for everyone, they weren't armed and they backed off when Turk reached them, but by the time the cops got here, there were a dozen of them, and a pissed-off dog and a nine-mil wasn't going to hold them off for much longer."

"You pulled your weapon on them?" Faith asked.

"Well, what the hell was I supposed to do?" Michael shouted back. "Say pretty please and bat my eyelashes at them?"

"Where's Marcus?" Faith asked.

"Inside," Michael said, "with two uniforms. I stayed out here because Turk wouldn't leave with these guys going crazy."

Faith turned to Turk. "Turk, come," she commanded.

Turk looked at Faith, looked back at the mob, then followed Faith without further hesitation. Michael shook his head and muttered something, but Faith was already too far ahead to hear him.

She walked inside and found Marcus sitting at his kitchen table, huddled over a cup of tea. His eyes were wide and staring, and Faith felt a rush of compassion for him. The two uniforms—big, burly men with bricklike jaws and tree trunks for legs—nodded seriously at her.

"Has anyone approached the house?" she asked the men.

"No," the younger-looking of the two men responded. "Not since we arrived."

"Did anyone present a weapon?" she asked.

"No," the other officer said. "No weapons."

Faith asked a few more questions, not because she needed the answers, but because she wanted Marcus to hear that they were handling the situation, and as angry as his neighbors wanted to get, they wouldn't be able to hurt him.

His neighbors. God, they were his *neighbors*. What the hell was wrong with this place?

It's supposed to be different.

"They want me out," Marcus said.

Faith blinked and turned to him. His eyes had lost that staring look, but they were still wide with fear in spite of the kind smile Marcus wore.

"I figured it would happen sooner or later," Marcus said. "After all, I'm a convicted murderer. I've changed, of course, but they wouldn't know that, and they wouldn't believe it if they did. I figured I could make it a while by keeping a low profile and filling my days with good deeds, but I knew they'd find me eventually."

"They will *not* get inside this housed," Faith promised.

"Oh not now," Marcus said, "But they will eventually. Police and FBI can't be here all day every day, can you?"

Faith didn't answer. She didn't need to.

"It's all right," Marcus said. "I accept the consequences of my actions."

"This is *not* your fault!" Faith insisted.

"I know it's not," he said. "But it's a consequence anyway."

"We can arrange protection," Faith said. "We can press charges against the rioters. These officers all have bodycams, we can present the footage in court, and—"

Marcus lifted his hand. "Do you know why people live in neighborhoods like this, Miss Bold?"

After what Faith had seen so far, she very much meant it when she replied, "I don't."

Marcus's smile widened slightly. "They live here to hide. They come here to pretend that all the filth and grief and violence of the world outside doesn't exist. They build matching houses and create fake meadows and forest paths. Ever notice that all the houses face away from the main road. That's intentional, Miss Bold. People live here because they want to pretend that the world is bright and beautiful and perfect, and they push out everything that suggests it might be otherwise. I'm something that suggests it might be otherwise, so they're pushing me out, and they won't stop pushing until I'm out, one way or another."

Faith didn't say anything for a while. The officers looked anywhere but at the stooped old man who'd just summed up the thoughts all three of them held even if they couldn't articulate it as well as Marcus had. The younger one shifted his feet. The older one coughed.

Faith finally said the only thing she could say, which of course, was the most useless thing to say. "I'm sorry. I'm so sorry, Marcus."

Marcus's eyes widened again, this time in surprise. "Oh, don't feel sorry for me," he said. "I was hiding too."

***

Faith said nothing on the ride back to the hotel with Michael. Michael tapped the steering wheel every few minutes but made no sound otherwise. Even Turk was silent, sitting in the second row with his head on the center console and staring bleakly out the window.

When they got to the hotel, they went through the motions of ordering lunch and only after they had finished and made coffee did they finally talk.

"I guess a neighbor caught us visiting him and looked him up," Michael said. "Told his neighbor who told his neighbor and so on."

Faith nodded but said nothing. After a moment, Michael said, "I keep expecting it to be better. It's weird. My only personal experience with this neighborhood has been two dead bodies and an angry mob, but I still expect it to be better. Like this is just a fluke, like something out of a crime show or… I don't know." He chuckled. "I just thought I would see a bunch of mildly arrogant rich people who spend an inappropriate amount of time talking about traveling and expensive toys but otherwise generally happy, decent people. Annoying people, but decent. Instead… I mean, I've been to some seedy neighborhoods, but this… this is beyond anything I've ever experienced."

"It's supposed to be different," Faith said.

"Is that a terrible thing to say?" Michael agreed. "I hate to say it, but you look at a neighborhood like this, and you think yachts and yoga pants; you don't think murderers and a damned lynch mob."

"I keep asking myself," Faith said, "what is the connection between Ethan Somersall and Evelyn Vance."

"You mean other than the fact that they both lived in hell?" Michael said.

"Exactly," Faith replied. "That's the only thing they have in common. They don't talk to the same people, they don't go to the same places. The only thing that connects them both is that they live in Cedar Hills."

"So what, the neighborhood is killing people?" Michael asked.

"Does Cedar Hills have an HOA?" Faith asked.

Michael's eyes widened as he understood where Faith was going. "I believe they do," he said. "Dammit. We should have thought of that already."

"Hindsight is twenty-twenty, Michael," she said. "We have a lead now. Call the Miltons and see if you can figure out who the HOA board members are. See if anyone was particularly active."

While Michael dialed, Faith thought about what she had said earlier. *Hindsight is twenty-twenty.* That was true, but it was also true that they should have talked to the HOA immediately. Even if they had no reason to suspect the homeowners' association, the HOA in a community like this had the pulse of the neighborhood, and they should have been one of the first groups Faith and Michael talked to.

Hindsight was twenty-twenty, but she should have thought of that. She would have thought of that if she wasn't waking up most nights soaked with sweat.

She shook the thought from her head. She had more important things to worry about than the nightmares. Like whether the HOA would be helpful or whether they would want everything wrapped up and shoved under the rug now that they had a convenient scapegoat in Marcus Washington.

She would see someone about the nightmares after the case. She promised herself this and almost believed it.

CHAPTER TWELVE

Bonnie Milton answered on the third attempt. Michael assured her that it was all right that she missed his earlier calls, then asked if the Miltons were active in the homeowners' association.

"Wonderful," he said after a moment. "Are you guys active? No, you won't get in trouble if you're not active. Do you know who the chairman of the board is?"

After a moment, he reached for a pen and paper and said, "Can you spell that for me, please?"

Faith leaned forward and watched Michael write Laszlo Kovacs. She typed the name into NICBCS and found several charges of assault. Interestingly, only one of those charges was aggravated.

"Do you have his address?" Michael asked. He looked at Faith and Faith nodded. "No, that's all right. Thank you, Mrs. Milton." After a moment, he smiled tolerantly and said, "Thank you, Bonnie."

He hung up. "What do we got?" he said to Faith.

"Laszlo Kovacs, forty-eight, six-foot-one, two hundred ten pounds, blue eyes, blonde hair rapidly graying, somehow not attractive at all in spite of everything I've just mentioned."

"Thank you for that," Michael said drily. "Anything relevant to this case?"

She turned her laptop so Michael could see his rap sheet. He whistled. "Boy, Cedar Hills keeps rolling out the hits, doesn't it? Got an address?"

Faith said, "453 Elm Shore Drive."

"Elm Shore?" Michael asked. "Do elms grow on shores?"

"I don't think it matters, Michael," Faith said. "Turk!"

The dog got instantly to his feet.

"Let's go boy," she said. "We have a lead."

***

Laszlo waited outside the door to his office, his arms crossed imperiously. He scowled and it didn't surprise Faith at all to know he was occasionally rough with people.

“What took you so long?” he shouted as soon as they were inside the office. “For heaven’s sake, you should have come to me right away!”

Faith had thought the same thing only moments ago but hearing it from this arrogant brute of a man stung. “We’re here now, Mr. Kovacs,” she said icily, “Can you tell me where you were on Friday, June 18th?”

He looked at her as though she had sprouted a third leg. “Who gives a shit where I was?” he said, “We should be asking where the killer is. Why—” his eyes widened. “—Me? You think it’s *me?”*

He turned almost purple but managed to keep his voice even as he said, “I will submit to a polygraph to prove my innocence.”

Faith rolled her eyes. Michael said, “Please answer the question.”

“I was at home with my wife eating dinner and watching tv. Would you like to review the security tapes from my home for that evening?”

“That won’t be necessary at this time, Mr. Kovacs,” Faith said. “Were you a part of the riot that occurred this afternoon at 18011 Birch Lane?”

“I was not,” he said. “I agree with their statement, but I don’t approve of their methods.”

“Really?” Faith said. “That’s interesting. I have a pretty long rap sheet in my possession that suggests that you’re not above these methods at all.”

Kovacs reddened and said, “I’ve answered for my actions, and anyway, most of those complaints didn’t happen that way.”

“Sure they didn’t,” Michael said. “Did you know Ethan Somersall?”

Kovacs stared at Michael in amazement. “Oh my God,” he said. “You do think it was me.”

“We’re just asking if you know him,” Faith said. “Why are you so certain that we suspect you?”

“Oh come on!” he said, “It’s clear that you suspect me. It offends me that you suspect me and that the reason you suspect me is my passion for my community, but it’s clear you suspect me.”

“You drove your knee into Henry Watson’s stomach because he refused to cut his grass,” Michael said.

“I…” Kovacs reddened. “That was one time.”

“What are your thoughts on these murders?” Faith asked.

Kovacs looked at Faith like she was stupid. “What are *your* thoughts on these murders?” he asked. “I’m disgusted by them. To think that something like this would happen in Cedar Hills. Do you know why people live here, Special Agent?"

"To hide?" Faith answered.

"What?" Kovacs said, "No. They move here to live *well.* That's what Cedar Hills is all about. Living well. Living well with yourself, living well with each other. People live here to live *well*, not to be murdered and buried in their neighbors' backyards. It infuriates me!"

Faith and Michael exchanged a glance. If Kovacs was putting on an act, it was a good one. He was every bit the jerk his record indicated, but he wasn't betraying any of the anxiety or guilt she would expect if he were the perpetrator. She noticed that while Turk was alert and watchful of Kovacs, he didn't appear terribly concerned.

"This place is perfect," Kovacs continued, his face falling suddenly. "You know, it's just… Well, you've seen it; it's perfect."

"What have you seen?" Faith asked, genuinely curious to know what had led him to believe this place was perfect.

"Look around!" he said. "It's quiet, it's peaceful, it's beautiful, it's clean, everyone is polite and kind to one another, there's harmony, it's convenient to everything we need, and we don't have to go to the city for anything."

He said *the city* like it was a curse word and looked at Faith with contempt. "Not everyone sees the need to live well."

"You're the chairman of the HOA, right?" Michael asked.

Kovacs rolled his eyes exaggeratedly. "Three guesses," he answered.

Faith had enough. She stood and approached until she was inches from Kovacs's face. "Mr. Kovacs, I appreciate that you think this is beneath you. I also don't give a shit. So start answering our questions or we're going to have this conversation at the field office."

Kovacs's scowl deepened a moment. Then he sighed and said, "All right."

"Excellent," Faith said. "How well did you know Ethan Somersall and Evelyn Vance?"

"By sight only," he said. "Neither of them were very active in the HOA." His lip curled down when he said that, as though he couldn't imagine a more serious crime. "Ethan followed the rules well enough. So did Evelyn Vance. She cheated on her husband I hear. Perhaps you should interrogate her boyfriend."

"Ah yes. The illustrious Beau Carpenter," she said. "Tell me about him."

"He's also passionate about the community, but he's far more aggressive than I am. He was one of the three men who first arrived at Marcus Washington's house this morning. I had to remove him from the HOA's board after multiple accounts of threatening people for violating the rules."

Faith and Michael exchanged a glance. "Did he ever mention either of the victims?" she asked.

"No," Kovacs replied. "Why do you ask?"

"No reason," Faith said.

She turned to Michael and gestured for the three of them to leave.

On their way out, Kovacs called. "This doesn't happen here."

"It already has," Faith replied.

They reached Beau Carpenter's house just before sunset. As they walked up, Faith wondered why on Earth Evelyn had been interested in a man like Beau Carpenter.

Michael knocked on the door, and when Beau answered, Faith understood immediately why Evelyn was interested in him. Beau Carpenter looked like he'd walked off the front page of a romance novel. He was shirtless, and his muscles were sculpted and unfairly symmetrical. He had a strong jaw that sat underneath piercing blue eyes and wavy blonde hair.

He smiled, and his teeth were, of course, perfect and white. But of course, he wasn't perfect, was he? He only looked perfect.

"Can I help you?" he asked in a voice that was the perfect balance of richness and huskiness.

"Special Agent Faith Bold," Faith said. "This is Special Agent Michael Prince. Can we come in?"

"Of course," he said.

He stepped aside and gestured for them to pass.

"After you," Michael said.

Beau's smile widened, but there was hardness behind those eyes. "Right," he said.

Turk growled low in his throat, and Faith realized that Carpenter was the first truly dangerous person they had interacted with in this neighborhood.

Carpenter looked at Turk and chuckled, then turned and walked inside the house. He led them to a large living room decorated beautifully with modernist furniture and a gas fireplace. "Y'all want a drink?" he asked.

"No thank you," Faith said.

"You, bro?" he said to Michael.

"I'm good, bro," Michael deadpanned.

Carpenter shrugged and opened the fridge. Turk tensed and Faith's hand flew to her shoulder holster, but when Carpenter came back out, he only had a beer. He cracked it with one hand and took a sip, then said, "What can I do for you, Special Agents?"

"Can you confirm your whereabouts on the night of Friday, June 18th?"

"Sure can," he said, "I was at the Phillies game."

Faith felt her spirits sink. "And you can prove that?"

"Sure can," he said. "My sister emailed me a video of me on the screen at the game. Would you like to see it?"

"We would," Michael said. "We would also like to know where you were after the game."

"I was in the Providence Motel," he said.

"Alone?" Faith asked.

He chuckled. "No."

"Who were you with?"

"I don't know, some chick from the game."

"Not Evelyn Vance?" Faith asked.

"No. Look, why don't you watch the hotel's security footage? The chick I was with was blonde; Evie was a redhead. I'm sure you've looked at my record, so I won't pretend I'm a boy scout, but I didn't kill Evie."

"We'll follow up with the hotel," Faith said. "Can you tell me how your relationship with Evelyn Vance ended?"

He smiled, "Simultaneously."

Faith decided he wasn't that attractive after all. "So it was a mutual parting of ways?"

"Very mutual."

"That's interesting," Faith said, "because when we pulled Mrs. Vance's phone records, your replies gave the very strong impression that you were unhappy with the way things ended."

Beau's smile faded. "You pulled my phone records?"

"Not yet," Michael said. "We pulled hers. Why? Something you want to tell us?"

"Not really."

"Well, that's too bad," Faith said, "because you're looking pretty good for her murder right now. If I were you, I would start telling me everything that could make you look a little less suspicious."

Beau sighed. "Look, I…" He lifted his arms and let them drop. "I guess Evelyn was special. I usually… well, emotions aren't really important to me, if you know what I mean."

"We follow," Faith replied, "but your relationship with Evelyn was more than just sexual."

"Well, I thought it was," Beau replied. "I guess I was wrong. It doesn't matter, though. Yeah, I tried to get her to stay with me—"

"You threatened her," Michael corrected.

"I didn't threaten her!" he said. "You know what? Pull my phone records. The last time we hooked up, she called me. We talked, and she explained that she loved Derek and while she loved what we had, it was time for it to end. I wasn't happy about it, but I agreed to drop it and leave her alone. You can hear it all. Also, it was her idea to have one last night together, and believe me, she left happy."

"We'll follow up on the phone records," Faith said. "For your sake, I hope they corroborate your story."

"They will," Beau said. "Particularly the part where I say, 'All right, Evelyn. If that's what you really want, then I'll back off. Sorry for freaking out on you, won't happen again,' and she replies with, 'Look, don't feel bad. While it lasted, it was fun, and I won't lie, you gave me something Derek never has. How do you feel about giving it to me one last time?'"

"Thank you for the preview," Faith said drily. "Like I said, we'll follow up. In the meantime, can you tell me how you knew Ethan Somersall?"

"Who?"

"Ethan Somersall. Forties, balding, touch overweight. Ring a bell?"

Carpenter chuckled again. "There's a lot of dudes here who look like that."

"Well, I'm asking about one dude."

"Well, I don't know Ethan Somersall. I'm not exactly sure how to prove that one. Maybe go through my texts and emails? Check my trash? Call my parents?"

"Keep up the attitude," Michael said. "That always helps."

He rolled his eyes and lifted the hand that wasn't holding the beer a few inches before letting it drop. "Look man, I didn't kill anyone, okay? I wasn't here."

"If you say so," Faith said.

She stood to leave. “That’s it for now, Mr. Carpenter, but do us a favor and stick around. We might have a few more questions after we check on those alibis.”

“I’ll be in town,” Beau said. He grinned at Faith and said, “Maybe after you convince yourself I’m not a murderer, we can grab dinner sometime.”

Faith didn’t dignify that with a response.

***

They checked. It checked out. Beau Carpenter wasn’t their killer.

Faith leaned back in her seat and stared at the car’s roof. Michael sighed and started the engine. “Well,” he says, “Maybe we can arrest him for being a prick.”

Faith shook her head. “We’re missing something.”

“We’re missing everything, Faith,” Michael said.

“No,” she replied. “We aren’t. We have almost everything, we’re just missing the connection. We know that they all live in the neighborhood, but we don’t know why that matters.” She fell silent a moment, then said, “There has to be a connection.” After another moment, she said, “I want to go back to Ethan Somersall’s house. I want to talk to Martha again. Everyone here has secrets. I want to know what Ethan’s are.”

Michael turned the car around and headed back to the Somersall’s house. “You want me to occupy the kids while you talk to Martha?” he asked.

“Yes,” Faith said.

“Well, then we’re stopping for ice cream sandwiches.”

“You sure you don’t just want an ice cream sandwich?”

“I’m sure that the kids are going to put two and two together when they see the FBI agents coming back to talk to their mother.”

Faith knew Michael was right. She wasn’t ready to suspect Martha just yet, but if her story didn’t check out, then she was going to start looking less like a grieving wife and more like an aggrieved wife. It would be better for everyone if the kids were shielded from that until they knew for sure one way or the other.

“All right,” she said, “ice cream it is.”

CHAPTER THIRTEEN

Martha opened the door just a crack when they arrived. She looked between the two agents and said, "Did you learn something about Ethan?"

Faith decided to be frank with her. "I'm hoping to learn something from you, Mrs. Somersall. I don't think you were completely honest with me the last time we spoke."

Martha's eyes widened, and Michael added, "What my partner means to say is that she feels you were concerned your children might hear something you don't want them to. So I brought ice cream sandwiches, and, if it's all right with you, I'd like to share them with your kids and give you a chance to talk to my partner in private."

Martha looked back and forth between them, clearly trying to think of a way to get rid of them. Faith said, "Special Agent Prince is right. I apologize for being unclear. We don't suspect you of wrongdoing, certainly not of involvement in your husband's or anyone else's murder. To be frank, Mrs. Somersall, I believe that there is a connection between your husband and Evelyn Vance, and I believe that the information you're withholding from me could help establish that connection."

Behind Martha, a voice called, "Mom? Who's at the door?"

Martha looked over her shoulder, then back at Faith. "I'm sorry, Special Agent. Now isn't a good time. If I think of anything, I promise I'll call, but…"

She stared to close the door, but Faith put her hand out. "Mrs. Somersall," she said evenly, "I can do this the hard way. I don't think you're a criminal, and I don't anticipate unearthing anything that might change that assumption, but I do anticipate unearthing something that you very much don't want your children to know. All I'm asking for is a few minutes of your time."

"For what?" Martha practically hissed.

"Mom!" the voice called.

Faith heard footsteps approaching and Martha turned around and said, "I'll be right there! Go watch tv with your brothers!" To Faith, she said, "I can't help you, Special Agent."

She moved to close the door again and Faith said, "He's not going to stop, Mrs. Somersall. Whoever's doing this. He's going to keep killing people. Whatever prompted him to kill your husband and Evelyn Vance will motivate him to kill again. At the moment, we don't know who he is, and the longer it takes us to find him, the greater the chance that he'll end up killing again. Maybe you. Maybe your kids."

Martha regarded Faith with an expression of naked hate that Faith took in stride. It wasn't Faith she hated. It was the fact that she couldn't hide anymore. The door to her closet had been opened, and it was only a matter of time before the skeletons fell out.

"I just want this to go away," she whispered.

"I know," Faith said. "We do too."

Martha sighed heavily then opened the door. "Kids!" she called. "The nice FBI agents have treats for you!"

There was a pitter-patter of little feet and the Somersall children crowded the agents. Faith looked at the bright smiles of the younger kids and the slightly sadder smiles of the older kids and wished that she could simply have left the family to pick up their lives in peace.

But then, she wasn't the one responsible for breaking their lives. That person was still out there.

The kids immediately squealed and ran toward Turk, who endured their aggressive affection with the tolerance of a saint.

"You have a dog?" a boy of about eight or nine asked, his tone suggesting that it was the most amazing thing he'd ever heard of.

"He's so cute!" a slightly older girl said, clasping her hands in front of her and beaming at Turk.

"Can we feed him?" another boy asked.

"Does he do tricks?" one of the older girls asked.

"All right!" Martha called. "Kids, with Special Agent Prince!"

"Aww, but we want to play with the dog!" the eight- or nine-year-old whined.

Michael held up the box of ice cream sandwiches like it was the Pied Piper's flute and the kids followed as readily as the ones in the fairy tale did, forgetting momentarily about Turk in their excitement for ice cream.

"Are you really a prince?" the youngest child, who might have been five or six, asked.

Michael smiled. "It's a secret," he said. "But I suppose I could share it over ice cream."

The younger kids cheered and the older kids tried vainly to hide their own interest in what Faith was sure would be a riveting tale. When they disappeared into the living room, Faith turned to Martha. Martha's arms were folded tightly over her chest and her lips were thin to the point of invisibility.

"Would you like to go to the kitchen?" Faith suggested.

Martha turned and led Faith wordlessly to the kitchen. When they arrived, she asked, "Would you like something to drink?"

"I'm all right," Faith said. "Thank you,"

"Well, I would," Martha said.

She opened a cupboard and retrieved a half-full bottle of vodka. She got a whiskey glass from the rack next to the sink, unscrewed the lid and poured it until the liquid half-filled the glass. Faith wondered if this habit was new or if Ethan's death had only hastened a slide that had begun years ago.

Martha opened the window and explained, "So the kids don't smell the alcohol."

Faith decided not to mention that the kids—the older ones at least—would almost certainly smell it on her breath.

Martha sipped generously and then put the lid back on the vodka and replaced it in the cabinet. She took another sip and leaned against the counter. She hadn't sat and hadn't offered Faith to sit, so they both stood while Faith waited for Martha to speak.

"You know, parents always say you should marry up." She looked Faith up and down and said, "Maybe not all parents, but mine sure did. 'Marry up,' they said. 'Find a doctor or a lawyer or an executive.' Well, I took their advice."

She took another sip of her vodka, grimacing in equal parts pleasure and pain as the warm liquid trickled down her throat. Faith wondered how long it would be before there was no more pleasure, only need.

"Ethan was hot," she said. "Smoking hot."

Her words were already starting to slur, and Faith decided that this wasn't her first drink of the evening.

"I mean," Martha continued, "he was average looking, but he was confident. You know, he'd walk into a room, and he was the star no matter where he was. That confidence, that self-assurance, that's the best aphrodisiac you could ever have."

Faith didn't say anything as Martha took another sip. "For the first five years, I thought I was Bonnie, and he was Clyde. He founded the firm with George Porter fifteen years ago, a year before Micah was born. Both of their names are on the sign, but Ethan was the real leader. He pushed George to take risks, to take the cases that no one wanted, to push for results when other firms just took their settlements and called it a day. I thought I was on cloud nine. And I was. For a while, I was happy as could be."

"But you know how it goes. I had kids, and my priorities changed. Suddenly, I didn't want to be Bonnie. I wanted to be Carol Brady, and Ethan… well, Ethan still wanted to be Clyde."

She took another sip and swirled the remaining liquid in the glass before continuing. "I used to blame him. I suppose part of me still does. It's always the men who push for more, isn't it? They're never satisfied with what they have. Sometimes it's wealth. Sometimes it's toys—cars, boats, airplanes. Sometimes it's women. Sometimes it's power. Sometimes they don't know what it is. They just always want more. And we argue with them and plead with them and ask them to stop, but they don't and you know what, Agent? We're just as guilty as they are because when we see that pretty little necklace in the window, we don't ask for it, but we let them know how pretty it is, and how we've always loved the way pearls look."

She took another sip and when she saw her glass was empty, she set it on the counter. "Have you heard the name Beau Carpenter?" she asked.

Faith's ears perked up. She managed to keep a calm demeanor as she asked, "How did your husband know Beau Carpenter?"

"He represented him," Martha said. "Eight years ago. Beau beat his girlfriend at the time so badly that the doctors said she was barely recognizable as human. She needed thirty rods in her face just to make her cheeks look straight. Anyway, the light of my life decided that the only way to get his lovely client off was to convince the girl to drop the charges. And he did. I'm not supposed to know how he did it, but what I'm not supposed to know is that he showed up to the hospital with pictures of her doing cocaine with Beau and told her that if Beau went to court, those pictures would go to court and he—Ethan—would make sure that everyone knew the drugs were her idea. It didn't matter if it was true or not."

Faith kept her voice calm, but inwardly she was bursting with excitement. This was it. This was the connection.

"I ate dinner with him," Martha said, her voice barely a whisper. "I let him play with my children." She looked up at Faith and the hate was back. "And now you know, Special Agent. Now you know the skeleton I hid in my closet. Did that help you find your murderer?"

"I think it may have," Faith said. "Thank you."

"Well, there's that at least," Martha said. "Have a nice day, Special Agent."

Faith turned and drew in a breath to call for Michael but stopped when Turk stiffened suddenly. She looked down at him and frowned. "Did you hear something, boy?"

Turk looked out the kitchen window toward the backyard and Faith's blood ran cold.

"What is it?" Martha asked. "What does he see?"

Turk bolted suddenly, rushing from the kitchen and nearly colliding with Michael on his way out the door. "What the—hey?" he said, just managing to avoid swearing in front of the kids.

Faith rushed past him, calling over her shoulder, "Keep the kids inside!" as she followed Turk.

Turk stopped at the front door and barked feverishly. Faith rushed to him and opened the door, and the moment it was open, he sprinted outside. Faith followed him around the house to the side yard. Turk stopped next to the fence that separated the Somersall house from their neighbors, across from the kitchen window, and began to dig feverishly.

Faith stopped just behind Turk and waited. She knew already what Turk had found. A moment later, she heard footfalls and turned to see Michael pull to a stop next to her. "Martha's inside with the kids. What is it?"

Just as he asked that, Turk barked and backed up, revealing a woman's hand, still stiff with rigor, poking out of the dirt.

"Oh Christ," Michael said.

"Call the sheriff," Faith said. "We have a third victim."

CHAPTER FOURTEEN

The police arrived ten minutes after Michael's call, led by Sheriff Morton. When he saw the body, he seemed more upset than surprised. "How the hell did we miss this?" he asked a morose Sergeant Anglesey.

"We focused on the public spaces," Anglesey said. "The judge wouldn't issue warrants for the residences."

Morton chuckled mirthlessly. "Well, do me a favor. Call him and tell him we found a body in the side yard of another residence. Tell him if he doesn't issue warrants for the rest of the houses, we'll just say probable cause and start looking anyway."

Anglesey hesitated. "Sir, it's after ten o'clock. Judge Garland won't be happy about being interrupted this late."

"Do I look like I give a shit?" Morton shouted. "Call him now, Anglesey, or do you need me to do it for you?"

"I'll call him, sir," Anglesey replied, wisely choosing not to argue further.

Morton removed his hat and ran a hand through his thinning hair. He looked at the body, surrounded by CSIs, and shook his head. "Goddammit," he said.

Faith could tell Morton wasn't used to being frazzled like this. For him to react the way he did meant that this case was stumping him too. That didn't make Faith feel any better about her own confusion.

"Who found the body?" Morton asked her.

"Turk did," Faith said. "He smelled it from inside the house."

"He smelled it from inside the house?" Morton asked incredulously.

"Mrs. Somersall had the kitchen window open," Faith explained. "The wind must have changed and blown the scent inside."

"Yeah, or he smelled the victim inside the house and smelled the same scent outside," Morton said. "Where's the family?"

"They're inside," Faith replied. "With a few uniforms."

"I want to talk to them," Morton said.

He started toward the house, but Michael laid a hand on his arm. Morton stopped and turned to him, eyes wide in shock. Faith could tell he wasn't used to having his decisions challenged.

"You can talk to them," Michael said, "but they're not the ones responsible."

"How the hell do you know that already?" Morton asked.

"They were visiting Martha's parents in Inglewood yesterday," Michael said. "Didn't get back until this afternoon."

"Who told you that?"

"Brock," Michael said, "the oldest son."

"And you believe him?" Morton challenged.

"I called the grandparents," Michael said. "They confirmed it."

"So? Maybe they killed her the day before."

"Maybe," Michael allowed, "but rigor rarely exists past twenty-four hours after death. I don't think it's likely that our victim was killed any time before last night."

Morton sighed and removed his cap to run his hands through his half-bald pate again. "Well, I'm going to talk to them anyway. Maybe they didn't kill her, but they sure as shit know her if she's on their property."

"The Miltons didn't know Evelyn Vance," Faith said.

Morton turned to her and said, "You mind if I go ahead and do my job, Special Agent? I know this is your show, but maybe they do know the victim and maybe talking to them will tell us something. Maybe it won't but it's better than sitting out here seeing how far we can stick our thumbs up our asses."

Faith lifted her hands in a placating gesture and Morton replaced his hat and stormed off. Faith and Michael watched him go, and Michael said, "He's not used to losing."

"We haven't lost yet," Faith said.

"No," Michael agreed, "but you have to admit there's starting to be a fourth quarter feel to this whole thing."

"It ain't over 'til the fat lady sings," Faith said.

"That's opera," Michael said.

"Actually, the phrase was coined by a sportswriter," Faith corrected.

Michael frowned at her, "What are you, Wikipedia?"

"Never mind," Faith said, "I'm just saying we can't let our emotions get the better of us."

"Well, thank you for that, Dr. Phil," Michael said. "I'll try to be more sanguine about the two-a-week serial killer we've stumbled on and have no idea who it is."

"On the contrary," Faith said. "We do have an idea who it is."

"Who, Beau Carpenter?" Michael said. "He wasn't in town for Evelyn, and Ethan's the reason he wasn't in jail. Maybe he kills Ethan to keep things hush-hush, and he had motive for Evelyn, but he wasn't there. We have pictures of him at the game when she was killed."

Faith didn't answer. She hated to admit it, but Michael was right. There was a connection between Evelyn, Beau, and Ethan, but you couldn't kill someone from a distance.

"Maybe he had her killed," Faith suggested. "It's worth following up on."

"Yeah, it is," Michael agreed. "Just like every other dead end we've followed."

Faith didn't have a response for that.

They fell silent and watched the growing crowd of onlookers craning their necks for a chance to see the latest victim.

"Christ, they're like vultures," Michael said, staring at the crowds as they milled around just outside the police cordon. "God, do they have nothing better to do? For fuck's sake, this could be them next week."

"That's not funny, Michael," Faith said.

"I'm not laughing," he replied. "It's like we're back in the dark ages or something. People have nothing better to do than to watch the latest public execution."

"Forget about it," Faith said. "Let's go talk to forensics and see what they know."

She and Michael walked to the freshly dug grave. Turk followed, and when he saw Baker, he barked a greeting. Baker offered a half-hearted smile and ruffled his fur when he trotted up to her, but when she looked up at Michael and Faith, her smile disappeared. "This one's fresh," she said. "Less than twenty-four hours old. Still stiff."

"I don't suppose we have an ID for this one, do we?" Michael asked.

"Actually, we do," Baker said. "Ariana Gonzalez, thirty-nine, married to Dominic Gonzales, forty-three. Cedar Hills residents, of course. 16805 Rosewood Place."

"Has anyone contacted the husband?" Faith asked.

Baker shrugged. "I assume so. That's the uniforms' job. I've been told I'm too descriptive when I call families."

"How did she die?" Faith asked, gesturing to Ariana.

“The official answer is pending autopsy; ask the Rabbi when he’s done. Unofficially, same as the others. Hit real hard upside the head, dead before she hit the ground or not long after.”

“The weapon?” Michael asked.

Baker sighed. She seemed genuinely tired rather than frustrated. “Same as the last one. Something blunt and heavy but not sharp. Maybe a baton or a sap. Something with a hard core but a soft outside. The skin doesn’t appear to be broken, but again, officially you need to ask the coroner.”

“Anything else we should know?” Faith asked her. “Anything at all that might indicate why she was killed?”

Baker sighed. “Well, I hate to speak ill of the dead, but between you and me, women don’t dress like that unless they don’t plan to be dressed for very long.”

Faith glanced at Ariana’s short skirt and low-cut halter top. From this angle, she could see a generous glimpse of red lace underneath the skirt and a hint of matching red lace under the halter top.

“So hubby’s out of town and Mrs. Gonzalez entertains a man friend,” Michael said. “Why am I not surprised?”

“We need to talk to Beau again,” Faith said to Michael. “I know he has a good alibi for Evelyn, but we know he knew Ethan and we know he sleeps around. We at least need to find out if he knows Ariana.”

Michael nodded. “You’re right. I’ll give him a call.”

The two of them thanked Baker, and the CSI gave Turk another friendly ruffle before turning back to join her team. Michael stepped behind the house to hear over the noise and Faith followed, signaling for Michael to put the phone on speaker.

Beau answered on the first ring. “Why hello,” he said. “Checking to make sure I’m still in town?”

“We’re coming over,” Michael said. “We found another body. Killed last night. Cheating on her husband. Ring any bells?”

“Well,” Beau said, “I’m sleeping with three married women at the moment, but only one of them lives here, and I wasn’t with her last night. I have some pictures to prove exactly who I was with last night, but I don’t know if it’s legal for me to show them to you.”

“What’s her name?” Faith asked.

“Candace DeGroot,” Beau replied. “Much prettier than her name suggests.”

“Can you describe—God, Carpenter, I didn’t ask for the damn pictures.”

“Well, I didn’t ask to be accused of murder,” Beau said smoothly. He dropped the suaveness and added, “Look, Special Agent, I’m over this, okay? I’m not Mr. Rogers, but I’m not Jack the Ripper either. I sleep around, and I knocked a few girls over the head when I was younger, but I don’t do that anymore, and I don’t kill people. You want to ruin Candace’s marriage to prove to yourself I’m not the killer? Go ahead. You want to arrest me and interrogate me until you’re blue in the face? Go ahead. I’m at home right now, and I’m staying here. You want to come get me? Come get me. I just want this to stop, so harass me to your heart’s content until you’re sure I’m not your guy.”

“We’ll think about it,” Michael said.

He closed his phone, closing with it a picture of Candace DeGroot enjoying a particular act with Beau Carpenter much more than her husband would appreciate knowing. They walked back to the scene just in time to see Morton walk out of the Somersall house. He saw the two of them and waved them over. When they reached him, he said, “The victim’s husband just touched down. He’s on his way to the coroner’s. CSI’s wrapped up here, so we’ll have his wife ready for him to identify when he arrives. I figured you want to talk to him, so you can either ride with us or follow us.”

“We’ll follow you,” Michael replied.

“Anything helpful from Mrs. Somersall?” Faith asked.

Morton shook his head. His earlier bullishness was gone. Now he simply looked defeated. “No. Nothing. She fingered Beau Carpenter, but we’re already watching him. He was at another resident’s house last night. Showed up at nine o’clock and didn’t leave until eight this morning.”

“So we’ve heard,” Michael said.

“You talked to him already?”

“He was involved with Evelyn Vance,” Faith said, “and Ethan Somersall was his defense lawyer.”

Morton’s eyes widened. “Damn. He was our guy up until this dead body showed up and had nothing to do with him.”

“We’re still not sure about that,” Faith said. “But we are sure that he has an alibi for each of the killings.”

“So he has an alibi for every event, but a connection to two of them, and possibly all three?” Morton asked.

“That about sums it up,” Michael said.

Morton nodded. “I’ll have Anglesey bring him in. It seems ridiculous that he would hire a hitman to kill people he had beef with, but this whole neighborhood is ridiculous. You guys can head to the coroner's if you want. I'll keep Carpenter awake until you guys are ready for him. You know where the sheriff's station is?"

Michael shook his head, and the sheriff gave him the address. That done, Michael, Turk and Faith headed for their car, escorted by the same two massive officers who protected Marcus Washington from the last mob.

On the way there, Michael asked, "You think Beau hired a killer?"

"Honestly?" Faith said. "No. He's narcissistic, but he's not insecure. If he's gonna kill someone, he's gonna kill them in person in a fit of rage, not from a distance after holding a grudge, and definitely not by hiring someone else to do his dirty work. We'll talk to him again and answer the question once and for all, but no, I don't think he's the guy."

"Yeah," Michael said, "me either."

They passed the rest of the drive to the coroner's office in silence. Faith looked out the window and played the key phrase over and over in her mind.

It's supposed to be different.

What was supposed to be different? Once more, Faith felt sure that if she knew the answer to that question, she would know the solution to the case, or at least where to look for it.

But she didn't know the answer, and time was running out. Ariana Gonzalez had been killed less than twenty-four hours ago and buried in the yard of another murder victim's family while police, the sheriff, and FBI agents actively investigated.

Their killer, whoever he was, was fearless and his behavior was escalating. Faith gave it two days tops before they had another victim on their hands.

It's supposed to be different.

"It never is, though, is it?" Faith said out loud.

"What?" Michael asked.

"Nothing," Faith said. "Just thinking out loud."

She stared out the window at the lights of the city as they drove.

CHAPTER FIFTEEN

They reached the coroner's office at eleven-fifteen. Cantor himself was fifteen minutes behind them with the body. Morton told the front desk to stall Mr. Gonzalez if he arrived before the coroner, then asked Michael and Faith if they wanted coffee.

"I'll take some," Michael said. "Thank you."

Faith nodded acceptance and the sheriff disappeared, returning a moment later with three steaming cups which he balanced with a dexterity surprising for a man his size. The three of them sat around a table in the small room used to receive people arriving to identify their loved ones. Turk crept under the table and laid down at Faith's feet, where he promptly fell asleep. Faith realized she was exhausted to the bone and took a big sip of her coffee.

They sat silently, all three of them too tired and frustrated to want to converse. Cantor arrived right on schedule and even he seemed subdued as he wheeled Ariana into the autopsy room and joined them. "Any word on Mr. Gonzalez?" he asked.

"Should be on his way," the sheriff said. "Might be having trouble getting through customs. He was coming from Spain."

"Well, at least we know it's not him, I guess," Cantor offered.

The other three weren't encouraged.

After a moment, Cantor said, "I'm going to get some coffee."

He disappeared and returned a moment later with a desperate-looking Hispanic man practically shoving his way past him. Morton, Faith, and Michael stood, and the noise woke Turk. All four of them entered the autopsy room just as Dominic tore the cover off of Ariana's body.

Cantor looked apologetically at Morton, but Morton waved him off. Dom was in no condition to cause problems after seeing his wife's body.

He stared at Ariana, his eyes as wide as dinner plates. He reached a trembling hand for her face, and Cantor began to tell him to stop when another wave from Morton quieted him.

He didn't end up touching her. His hand hovered a moment over her face without making contact. Then it drifted to meet the other on the crown of his head. Dom unleashed an ear-splitting shriek, then sank to his knees, staring in disbelief at his wife's body and repeating over and over in Spanish, *"No es possible, no, mi amor, no puedes estar muerta, Madre de Dios, no."*

He began to weep then, his shoulders shaking even before the first tears fell. He cried out again, and this time the tears came as he lowered his head to the ground like a prostrate sinner, weeping into the concrete floor of the autopsy room while the two agents, the sheriff, and the coroner watched.

After a moment, Turk walked up to him and laid his head over Dom's, but for once, Turk's comfort wasn't enough. Dom continued to wail as though Turk wasn't even there.

Michael looked at Faith and Faith nodded. The two of them walked quietly from the studio back to the reception room. A moment later, Cantor followed, then the sheriff. Morton kept an eye on Dom through the window, just in case he tampered with the body after all, but other than that, they allowed him his privacy as he grieved. Only Turk remained, his head resting on Dom's, his eyes shining with compassion purer than any human could feel.

Dom wept for fifteen minutes straight, and the clock on the wall read midnight when he finally got shakily to his feet. Cantor left the reception and spoke quietly to him for a moment. Faith didn't hear the exact words exchanged, but she could imagine them.

"Did she suffer?"

"We don't believe so."

"What happened?"

"We're not sure yet."

"Who did it?"

"We're working hard to find out."

"I love her."

"I'm so sorry, Mr. Gonzalez."

After five minutes or so, Dom allowed Cantor to lead him into the reception area. He looked ten years older than he did twenty minutes ago. Grief radiated from every pore of his being, and Faith felt a lump form in her throat. A glance at Michael showed he was similarly affected.

Death was like that. People said you got used to it in Faith's line of work, but you never really did. You got better at functioning when faced with it, but it never got easier to look into the eyes of a man whose reason for living had been bludgeoned to death by a serial killer.

Dom sat on the empty chair, Turk at his side. Cantor stood, his arms folded across his chest, his eyes fixed on the floor.

Faith almost hated how easily she fell back onto her training. "Mr. Gonzalez, I am so sorry for your loss."

Dom nodded vacantly.

"I'm so sorry to have to ask this," Faith continued, "but do you have any idea who might have wanted to hurt your wife?"

"You mean kill her?" Dom asked.

Faith nodded. "Yes," she said.

"No point in saying different," Dom replied. "It is what it is. My wife was murdered."

There was no emotion in his voice as he said it. He was only stating a fact, one that he would waffle between denying and accepting until she was lowered into the ground or else burned to ash and he was forced to finally accept once and for all that the love of his life was gone, never to return.

"Can you think of anyone who might have wanted your wife dead?" Faith asked.

Dom shook his head. "Ari? No, not her. She was a saint. I know husbands always say that about their wives, but she really was. Everyone loved her. She was a Sunday school teacher at our church. She would bake cookies for the kids and make little Valentine's cards for them. Christmas and birthdays too. She cared for her *abuelo* like a treasure, visited him every week until he died. She tried hard to get the state to allow her *abuela* to live with us, but they said she needed assisted living. Ari was looking into getting a studio apartment near the home to visit her."

Faith had no doubt about the apartment and had no doubt that the reason for the apartment was very different from the reason Dom believed. Knowing that the woman he thought he had lost was not the woman lying on the table almost hurt Faith more than if she truly had been a saint.

"How would you describe your relationship with your neighbors?" Faith asked.

"The Saint-Pierres and the Dominguezs?" Dom replied. "We loved them like family. Hector Dominguez is one of my best friends."

"And your wife?" Faith asked. "She got on well with them too?"

"Of course," Dom replied. "She's the one who introduced me to Hector and Xochitl. She knew Hector from work a long time ago."

"And where was that?" Faith asked. "The workplace, I mean?"

"Oh, some fast-food chain," Dom said, "Wendy's I think, or maybe Hardee's."

"And how long ago was a long time ago?"

"Oh, a long time. Twenty years, maybe."

Faith nodded. "And did your wife work currently?"

Dom's lip trembled. He pressed his fingers to his eyes for a moment, then pulled them away. "It's just hard. Was. Did. Knew. It's just hard to think of all of that as past tense now."

He took a breath and said, "Sorry. You were asking if she's working now. No, she isn't—wasn't working. We tried for a baby for a while, but that never happened either. I think that's why she loves—loved the kids at church so much. Oh God, how do I tell them?"

Michael spoke then. "Mr. Gonzalez, was your wife acting different lately?"

Dom's brow furrowed in confusion. "Different?" he asked. "Different how?"

"You tell me," Michael said. "Anything at all out of the ordinary."

"No," Dom said. "I mean, she was a little aloof with me after her *abuelo* died, but everyone grieves differently. She needed time to herself. I was going to cancel my business trip, but she told me to go. Said she needed space for a while. I respected her decision."

"And do you know of anyone who might have visited her while you were gone?"

"Sure," Dom said. "The Dominguezs and Saint-Pierres for sure. Pastor Julio and his wife, maybe some of the parents and kids from Sunday school."

Michael took a pen and notepad from his jacket. "Can you tell me the names of everyone you know for sure visited your wife?"

"I don't know anyone for sure," Dom said. "I'm just saying it wouldn't surprise me. Everyone loved her. She was a saint."

Michael put the pen and notepad back into his pocket. He exchanged a glance with Faith.

Faith nodded and stood, "Again, Mr. Gonzalez, I am so sorry for your loss. If you think of anything else, please call us."

She handed him a card, which he took without looking at it. "Oh, Ari," he moaned. "Oh, *mi amor.*"

He buried his face in his hands and cried softly. Morton stood, and he and the two agents nodded their goodbyes to Cantor and left with Turk.

***

Beau Carpenter waited in an interrogation room when the three of them arrived. The two huge officers from earlier—Coulson and Maguire, according to their name badges—stood on either side of him, their massive arms folded across their chests, their faces wearing glares that would make any drill sergeant tear up with pride.

Gone was the easy self-assurance. Gone was the smugness and pride. Away from his comfort zone and at the mercy of the law, Beau looked like a scared little boy. Faith had to admit it felt good to see him like that.

She and Michael entered and the uniforms left, casting a final stony glare at Carpenter on their way out.

Carpenter offered the two agents a weak smile. "Well, hello there, agents," he said, his voice thready and much older-sounding than before. "Here for round three?"

"Carpenter, I'll be honest," Faith said, "I don't think you did it."

"Really?" Carpenter said sarcastically. "Well, thank you so much for bringing me all the way down here to tell me that."

"Keep up the attitude," Michael said. "Like I told you earlier, it can only help."

Carpenter laughed bitterly. "There's no help. People like me have enemies and lovers, but no friends."

"Poor baby," Michael deadpanned.

"Like I said," Faith interjected. "I don't think you did it. The problem is that your name keeps popping up when we look into these victims. You dated Evelyn Vance, you hired Ethan Somersall—and lied about knowing him as well. We'll come back to that—and Ariana Gonzalez was buried in Martha Somersall's yard. The only common thread between the three victims is you."

Beau snorted. "That, and they all lived in Cedar "Hells." They were all pieces of shit in the same vein as me too. Maybe not as bad as me, but they weren't good people. Evelyn was cheating on her husband and at the risk of making you think I really did kill her, I'll bet Ariana was too."

"It might be better if you don't take risks," Michael offered.

Beau lifted his hands and let them drop. "I'm just saying, I'm not the only common thread. Just the best-looking one."

He was right, but Faith didn't let him see that. "I don't think you did it," she repeated. "But that's not enough. You need to start convincing me that you had nothing to do with their deaths."

"And pictures of me not there when they died aren't enough?" he asked.

"It's enough to prove you didn't pull the trigger," Michael said, "92but a guy like you must have friends. Maybe violent friends. Maybe friends who don't mind getting their hands dirty."

Beau chuckled bitterly. "Christ. Pull my phone records. Pull my emails. Fucking talk to my friends. I'm a womanizing douchebag and a *former* woman beater, not a killer. I've told you this I don't know how many times. I'm cooperating. Sorry I'm not kissing your ass doing it, but I'm cooperating."

"You're really bad at convincing us," Michael observed.

Beau lifted his hands and let them fall again. "I don't know what to say," he said. "And I'm tired of repeating myself. If you have any more questions, ask my lawyer."

Faith sighed. "So you didn't hire anyone to kill Evelyn Vance, Ethan Somersall, and Ariana Gonzalez?"

"What, like a mob hit?" Beau asked. "For God's sake. Why would I do that? Believe it or not, Special Agent, I like my life, *and* I'm not actually stupid enough to believe I can get away with killing people. I'm also not stupid enough to think I'd last a minute in prison. Am I wrong, Special Agent?"

Faith looked at his blonde hair, blue eyes, and surfer-boy body and said with complete sincerity, "No, you're not wrong."

"Well, there you go. A lot of people hate me, but I'm not among that crowd, and no one is worth becoming some tattooed Aryan Brotherhood widebody's bitch. Does that convince you, Special Agent? The fact that I like myself enough to not want to go to prison?"

"Actually, yes," Faith said. "It does."

She stood. "The police will be harder to convince, but you'll get to go home eventually. My advice? Make it your home for as short an amount of time as possible. Get out before Cedar Hills eats you too."

Beau laughed mirthlessly. "Smartest thing you've said all day."

The three of them left Beau then, nodding to Coulson and Maguire to resume their vigil. They said a brief goodbye to Sheriff Morton, then headed back to the hotel for what would be nothing more than a long nap at this point.

Once in the car, Faith said, "How long do you think they'll keep him?"

Michael shrugged. "Morton will go through his phone and emails like he said he would. That'll probably take until mid-morning tomorrow. He won't find anything, and I figure that'll piss him off enough that he'll sweat Beau another hour or two before sending him home." He glanced at Faith. "Why'd you tell him to leave?"

Faith shrugged. "I don't know. I don't pity him like I pitied Marcus. He disgusts me, actually. I guess Cedar Hills just disgusts me more."

Michael nodded. "Yeah, it has a way of doing that. So what are our next steps?"

"Good old-fashioned legwork," Faith said. "We interview the Dominguezs and the Saint-Pierres, Pastor Julio and the other church staff."

"I'll take the church," Michael said. "I could use a break from Cedar "Hells" as the lovely Mr. Carpenter so elegantly put it."

"Works for me," Faith said.

She could use a break herself if she were honest, but she wasn't ready to leave just yet. She still felt like the answer was right in front of her if she could only see it.

They reached the hotel and Faith fought her exhaustion as long as she could. She pored over her notes, desperate to find something, anything that could make a tapestry out of all of the disconnected threads they had.

Finally, though, her drooping eyelids overwhelmed her and she dragged herself reluctantly to bed. The one positive that came from her exhaustion was that she was too tired to dream, the only silver lining of a very dark cloud.

CHAPTER SIXTEEN

Faith woke early, not refreshed by her brief nap, but at least no longer bone-weary. Turk was as alert as always, seemingly unaffected by his long day yesterday. He alone of the three of them seemed to be in cheerful mood, wagging his tail happily as Faith and Michael took turns showering and dressing.

They enjoyed the hotel's complimentary breakfast, and Faith idly wondered what would happen to the producers of mini-muffins if hotels ever stopped buying from them. She recalled a speech given in a business seminar she attended ten years ago. She didn't pay much attention to the speech. She had only attended the seminar to try to get into the pants of a charming Harvard Business School student who mentioned to her that he liked women in uniform.

So, she came to the seminar in full battle fatigues, earning stares from the mass of students and executives in their Italian suits and Swiss wristwatches. The gambit paid off when Harvard grad turned out to be particularly adept once she removed the fatigues. Nothing came of the relationship, and after a few more dates, they went their separate ways amicably. They still talked on social media every now and then. He was a senior vice president at an aerospace firm. Married to a pretty engineer with three beautiful children.

The one part of the seminar she did remember was when the speaker quoted a business idol of his and asked the attendees where today are the makers of carburetors? The point of that was that the makers of carburetors made better and better carburetors but never thought to make anything different. Then one day, someone came up with the idea of fuel injection and suddenly the best carburetors on Earth were obsolete.

She wasn't sure why these idle thoughts occupied her, but she knew herself well enough to know that the answer would come to her eventually if she allowed it to percolate long enough. Her mind worked that way, teasing at the edges of a problem in her subconscious until the answer came suddenly, often violently, to her conscious mind.

She tested the earlier phrase she knew was critical to the case, *It's supposed to be different*, but the answer to that puzzle—if there was one, remained locked away in her mind. She dismissed it and finished her breakfast, helping herself to another one of the surprisingly satisfying tasteless muffins.

After breakfast, they parted ways. Michael went to Our Immaculate Lady of Hope Church to interview Pastor Julio. The church, despite its name, was Presbyterian, not Catholic. Faith considered idly that it was yet another example of something hiding its true character behind a front, then decided she was overthinking it.

She took Turk in the car at Michael's suggestion. It would be easier for him to catch a rideshare than a woman with a dog. She headed to the Gonzalez resident, parking across the street. She checked the database and learned that the house to the left was the Saint-Pierres' and the house to the right was the Dominguezs'. She decided on the Dominguez house first, since Dom seemed to suggest they were closer to that family.

The door was answered by a man around Dom's age, but taller and in better shape, his abs and arms clearly defined under his merino wool sweater. He had a neatly trimmed, close-cropped beard and thick, curly black hair that showed not a hint of gray. He was red-faced and puffy-eyed with tears and Faith knew immediately he was the man Ariana Gonzalez was cheating on her husband with.

The Sunday school teacher wife sleeping with the hot neighbor who was also her husband's best friend. It was like a caricature of a soap opera, which made perfect sense for this neighborhood.

"Good morning, Mr. Dominguez," Faith said, "I'm Special Agent Faith Bold with the FBI. I'd like to ask you a few questions about Ariana Gonzalez."

Hector Dominguez sniffed and wiped his eyes. "Uh, sure," he said, "Come in."

He led Faith inside to a living room that looked like every other living room in the neighborhood, albeit a little less lived-in than the Somersall place. Upscale furniture and an unnecessarily massive television dominated one wall and attractive decorations lined the shelves and walls—no doubt the doing of Mrs. Gonzalez.

"Xochitl!" Hector called. "Can you bring coffee?"

"That's all right, Mr. Dominguez," Faith said, "I've had coffee already."

"The coffee is for me," Hector said. "But would you like water?"

Faith accepted the water to avoid seeming rude, and Hector called to his wife again. A moment later, Xochitl walked into the living room.

If Hector was the male counterpart of Ariana, Xochitl was the counterpart of Dom, short and stout with a round face and small eyes set over a cute button nose. She offered Faith a forced smile as she set a glass of water on the coffee table in front of her.

When she handed her husband the coffee, her smile disappeared and her shoulders visibly tensed. Faith wondered if she knew of her husband's affair before Ariana's death or if it was her husband's reaction that clued her in.

"Mr. Dominguez, can you tell me how you knew the victim?" Faith asked.

Xochitl's shoulders tensed further, and when Hector said, "We were friends," she snorted softly.

Faith went through the boilerplate questions with both of them, but it was clear that Hector wouldn't speak honestly with his wife present, so after a few minutes, Faith said, "Mrs. Dominguez, would you mind if I spoke to your husband in private?"

Xochitl stiffened and flashed Hector a look of naked contempt. Hector didn't meet her eyes. Faith wondered if their marriage would end or, if like so many marriages, it would drag on until neither of them felt anything but hate for the other.

She offered Faith another forced smile and left without another word. When she was gone, Hector sniffed and said, "I didn't kill her. I know you need to ask that, and I know you know that I was… that we were… involved, so I know I'm a suspect, but I didn't kill her."

"Can you confirm your whereabouts two nights ago?"

Hector chuckled. "I was here. You can call my wife back in to confirm if you want. We spent the whole night arguing."

"May I ask about what?"

Hector looked frankly at her and said nothing.

"Right," Faith said. "Was Mrs. Gonzalez aware that your wife knew of the affair?"

Hector shook his head. "Xochitl only found out last week. Ari sent me a picture, and I forgot to delete it from my phone." He met Faith's eyes, and his own seemed to plead with her. "I'm not a bad man, Special Agent. I've been married to Xochitl for twenty years and haven't cheated on her once before now. It's just… things…" he lifted his hand and let it drop. "You know, when I met Xochitl, she couldn't get enough of me. There were days she wanted it so bad I couldn't walk after." He chuckled and smiled briefly. "I thought I was the luckiest man on Earth. But you know, life goes on. She started getting frigid the past few years. I did everything I could think of. I got in shape, I bought flowers, chocolates. I took her on dates, I gave her massages. It didn't matter. She just didn't want it anymore."

"Mr. Dominguez, I'm not here to judge your personal life. I need to know if you or your wife have any idea who might have killed Mrs. Gonzalez."

He shook his head. "Dom's the only person except my wife and I who would have a motive, unless she was sleeping with someone else's husband too. Even if Dom knew, he wouldn't kill her. He's a good guy."

Hector said that last with a hint of contempt, and Faith wasn't sure if it was directed at Dom or at himself.

Faith didn't want to be there anymore. She'd had enough of the soft white underbelly of Cedar Hills. "Can you confirm you and your wife's presence at home two nights ago?" she asked.

He shrugged. "I watched the fight on pay-per-view," he said, "You can confirm that with my cable provider. I mean, I could have just left it on and then went to kill her, but I don't really know how else to prove it."

"I'll take a look," she said. "Thank you for your time, Mr. Dominguez."

She left the house and headed for the Saint-Pierres, her skin crawling with revulsion. Just being here made her feel dirty, reminding her of her own deep dark secret.

The Saint-Pierres were equally unhelpful. Carolyn talked on and on about how sad it was that Ari was cooped up at the house all day with nothing to do and opined that it was no wonder she strayed. Jacques expressed his opinion that Hector was an egotistical bastard but not the type to kill.

"Can't stain his wool sweaters with blood," he said, laughing loudly at his joke.

Faith couldn't wait to leave. She called Michael on the way and learned that the church staff was as blissfully unaware of Mrs. Gonzalez's true nature as her husband was.

"Wonderful," she said. "Another dead end. Meet for lunch?"

"Works for me," he said. "I'll see you soon."

Faith hung up and against her will, her thoughts turned to her secret.

Let's see how you bleed, little girl.

"Fuck you," she muttered under her breath.

***

They were making better and better carburetors. They needed to start making fuel injectors.

She said that to Michael, and Michael—understandably—stared at her and said, "What?"

"We're interviewing resident after resident and each interview is a dead end. We need to expand our horizons."

"How do you mean?"

"We assumed that the killer was a resident because he knew the neighborhood and its inhabitants well, but it doesn't need to be a resident. A landscaper or contractor would know Cedar Hills, probably better than any of its residents."

Michael's eyes widened, "And there wouldn't need to be a connection between the victims. The contractor would be the connection."

"This could be our missing link," Faith said.

"I'll call Laszlo at the HOA," Michael said. "You open up the database and start feeding it names."

"At a public diner?" Faith said.

"Come on, Faith, figure it out," Michael said. "Tilt your screen down and turn the brightness low. Make sure you're not facing a security camera. Pretend you're a detective for Heaven's sake."

Faith smiled wryly at Michael's excitement. Later, she would give him grief for talking to her like this, but for the moment, she was grateful to see him excited about something.

And she was excited too. Later, she would have to deal with the fact that neither of them realized this earlier, and that would be hard; but for now, she was just happy to have something that felt like a real lead.

Michael got a hold of Laszlo, and after a brief conversation, told Faith that Laszlo was emailing a list of every landscaper, contractor and delivery person assigned to Cedar Hills. In a rare stroke of good luck, the database search was quick. They landed on a solid lead with the third name.

"Well, would you look at that," Michael said, leaning over her. "We have ourselves a peeping tom."

Richard Fenimore, thirty-one, was a seven-year veteran of the postal service. His route included Meadowbrook Heights, Applewood Villas, and nearly all of Cedar Hills, including the homes of all three victims along with the Miltons, Beau Carpenter, Laszlo Kovacs, and Marcus Washington. He had three priors, all of them counts of trespassing and harassment. Specifically, Mr. Fenimore enjoyed watching couples through their windows, bonus if those couples were in a state of undress.

Faith hated stereotypes, but Fenimore looked exactly like you'd imagine a peeping tom would look. He was five-foot-eleven, a blubbery two-eighty, and had prematurely balding tan hair and a weak jaw, topped with that peculiar style of wire-rimmed glasses that only seemed to be worn by rapists and serial killers.

Which Fenimore might very well be.

"You want to do the honors or shall I?" Michael asked.

"I'll call him," Faith said. "You settle the bill and call for a patrol car. I have a feeling we're going to need lights and sirens for this."

"Of course I'm the one stuck paying the bill," Michael groused. He wore a big grin, though, and quickly called for the check.

Faith called Fenimore and wasn't surprised to receive no answer. She left a message and called again, but again got no answer.

"All right," Michael said, "PD's on the way. Any luck?"

"No," Faith said, "but USPS has body cams now, don't they?"

"Body cams? No," Michael said, "but they do have dash cams, and those dash cams send a ping to the vehicle's home base. I'll call USPS while we wait for the car and see if they can help me track Fenimore."

"I'm sure they'll be more than happy to, once you remind them that they're still employing a convicted peeper," Faith suggested.

"Good point," Michael said.

By the time the patrol car arrived, they had a lead on Fenimore. He was on his route, but not in Cedar Hills. That was a plus as far as Faith was concerned. The last thing they needed was another circus. Michael told the owner of the diner that they would come back for their vehicle later and met Faith outside just as the patrol car arrived.

Anglesey was the driver. "Probably catch hell for this, but I'll be damned if anyone but me gets this collar. Well, other than you two, of course."

Turk barked and Anglesey said, "Sorry, you three."

"Go for it," Michael said. "I just want him in a nice, cozy cell."

"Let's not get ahead of ourselves," Faith cautioned. "We don't know for sure he's our guy."

"We know for sure he's a prick," Michael replied.

"Fair enough."

Anglesey hit the lights, and the car flew through the city streets. Faith tried Fenimore twice while they drove and received no answer either time.

They caught up with Fenimore just as he pulled out of Meadowbrook Heights. Anglesey hit the siren and pulled up behind the mail truck. He called for Fenimore to stop on his radio, and braced himself for the chase.

"He's not gonna stop," Michael said. "No way."

But he did. To the surprise of all three of them, the mail truck immediately put its hazards on and pulled to the side.

"Shit," Anglesey whispered.

"You think he's armed?" Faith asked.

"Wouldn't surprise me," Anglesey said. "Are you two carrying?"

Faith nodded, and Anglesey said, "All right. I'll approach the driver's side door. Special Agent Bold, you take the passenger side. Special Agent Prince, you remain in the vehicle and call for backup in case things get squirrelly. Let's hope—hold on."

Fenimore leapt from the passenger side of the mail truck and, with surprising dexterity, vaulted over a low iron fence into a backyard.

Anglesey looked at the two agents and said, "New plan. You three go after him. See if the dog can take him down. I'll follow in the car."

"Right," Faith said.

The three agents leapt out of the car. Turk immediately followed Fenimore, barking and leaping the fence like it wasn't even there. Faith followed as quickly as she could but Turk outstripped her, which was a good thing since Fenimore was apparently far more athletic than his bulk suggested.

He led them on a circuitous chase through the neighborhood, leaping fences and crossing yards, throwing down birdhouses, barbecues, and planters behind him as he ran.

He turned a corner and ran in between two houses, then climbed over a fence into a ditch. The fence was too tall for Turk to leap over.

"Dammit," Faith cursed.

She considered trying to throw Turk over the fence, but the dog weighed close to ninety pounds, and she didn't think she would be able to heft him over the fence without hurting him or herself.

She looked around, desperate for something to use, but it was Turk who finally spotted the old lawnmower through a hole in one of the fences. Faith quickly jumped the fence and opened the door. Turk ran past her in a blur, leaping on top of the lawnmower and from there over the fence.

Faith followed him, but by this time, Fenimore was gone. Turk ran as though he still had his trail, and Faith could only hope that he was right.

She followed him through the ditch until he leapt over another fence—this one low, thankfully—and Faith heard Fenimore yelp.

"Hold him, boy!" Faith shouted, sprinting to catch up.

Turk leapt for Fenimore, jaws snapping, but the man somehow managed to duck the blow and continued running.

"Dammit," Faith cursed again, following Turk as he chased Fenimore into the road and then over another fence on the opposite side. Behind her, Faith could hear Michael huffing and puffing and relaying their location to Anglesey. A twinge of pain started in Faith's left knee, and she gritted her teeth and fought through it, calling for Fenimore to stop.

Fenimore sprinted again for the road, right into the blaring sirens and flashing lights of Anglesey's patrol car. He skidded to a stop and tried to change direction and that's when Turk caught him, grabbing his leg and dragging him to the ground.

He released a high-pitched scream and began weakly slapping and punching at Turk, trying to dislodge him. Faith jogged to a halt a few yards away and said, "I'll call him off, but only if you stop resisting."

Fenimore glanced between the two agents and the police officer with wild eyes. For a moment, Faith thought he would ignore her warning, but Turk growled and he slumped backwards and raised his arms over his head.

"You move, and I'll tell Turk to aim in between your legs," Faith warned. "Got it?"

Fenimore bobbed his head feverishly up and down and Faith called Turk off. Turk released Fenimore's leg and growled at him.

"Call him off!" Fenimore squeaked. "You said you'd call him off!"

"He's off," Faith said. "He's probably just pissed that you punched him. Can't say I blame him. Fortunately for you, you punch like a child. If you had hurt him, I might not be able to stop him."

Fenimore gulped and stared fearfully at the growling shepherd.

"All right, creep," Anglesey said, cuffing Fenimore. "You're wanted for questioning regarding the murders of Evelyn Vance, Ethan Somersall, and Ariana Gonzalez." He yanked Fenimore roughly to his feet. "But you know that already, don't you?"

“What?” Fenimore said, “Murder?”

“In you go, track star,” Anglesey said, dragging him to the car and not-too-carefully pushing him inside.

Faith looked at Michael and nodded in satisfaction. Michael lifted a hand and Faith high-fived him. Then they both held their hands for Turk to shake.

Turk lifted both paws at once and Faith laughed. “Good dog,” she said.

CHAPTER SEVENTEEN

"Take your time," Michael said. "I have all day."

Fenimore sat with his hands shackled in front of him on the table. He trembled violently, and there was a suspicious stain in the front of his pants. A bandage covered his left calf from ankle to knee. Turk hadn't torn him up too badly, but Fenimore nearly passed out when he saw the blood on his leg, so Faith decided the overkill was worth it to keep him alert.

Funny how so many serial killers were squeamish when it came to their own blood.

"I told you," Fenimore squeaked. "I didn't kill anyone. I don't even know who those people are."

"Ooh," Michael said, clucking his tongue. "See, that was a mistake. You know why that was a mistake?"

"Please," Fenimore sobbed.

"Did your victims say please?" Faith asked. "Did they beg like you're begging?"

She leaned casually against the wall with her arms folded, and her voice never rose above a conversational tone, but her eyes were hard as diamonds, and her jaw was set dangerously. Fenimore gulped and his voice was barely a whisper when he said, "I didn't kill anyone."

"You didn't answer my question," Michael said. "That's a mistake too."

"I... I... I..." Fenimore stuttered.

"That's okay," Michael said, "I'll answer it. Saying you don't know Ethan Somersall, Evelyn Vance, and Ariana Gonzalez is a mistake because you're a shitty liar, Richard. Can I call you Richard?"

"W—what?"

"See, when you lie, you always gulp like you're swallowing something particularly hard. You have experience with that, Richard?"

"Please..."

"Never mind. Your left eye twitches too. Now when I asked you if you knew the victims and you said you didn't, you gulped and twitched like no one's business. So I'm going to ask you the question again, and if you lie to me again, I'm going to smear peanut butter on your crotch and tell Turk dinner is served. You get me?"

"Y—you can't touch me!" Fenimore shouted. He jutted his chin forward and stared at Michael with what he thought was defiance but looked a lot more like fright. "I have rights!"

"Well, so you do," Michael said. "All right. I'll tell Anglesey to go ahead and press charges. You have a lawyer you want to call or you need a public defender?"

"Charges?" Fenimore blinked.

"Of course," Michael said. "You're *suspecto primo*. We're going to charge you for multiple counts of trespassing, vandalism, and of course, murder. See you at your arraignment."

He turned to leave and Faith pushed away from the wall to follow him.

"Wait!" Fenimore cried.

They turned back to him, eyebrows raised.

Fenimore sighed and slumped forward in his seat. "Okay, I knew them," he said tonelessly. "But I didn't kill them, all right?"

His left eye twitched and Faith leaned forward. "Do yourself a favor," she said, "And start telling the whole truth now instead of waiting for the judge to ask."

He looked at her with his lip pooched out in a disgusting imitation of a child's pout. "I didn't kill them okay. I just… watched them."

"Watched them?"

"I watched them fuck, okay?" he practically shouted. "I… Look, in case you haven't noticed, I'm not exactly a supermodel. Women aren't exactly lining up to date me. I deliver people's mail every day, and I see all of these smoking hot women, and I don't even need to ask, you know? I don't need to wonder. They don't want me. They won't want me. If I get lucky, maybe one day I can save up and go to Vegas and stay at one of those bunny ranches, but other than that, I'm out of luck in the sex department."

He sat up and licked his lips. "So I watch people. I memorize the addresses of particularly attractive women and then I memorize their habits. I know when they're home, and when they're not. I know when they shower and when they dress. I arranged my route so I could see my favorites."

He smiled, and Faith's stomach turned. "Ariana was one of my favorites. She had such a smoking body. And that mouth." He whistled.

"Let me tell you, her neighbor is one lucky man. If I had a girl like that, I would spend all day naked."

As he recounted his exploits and the particular "specialties" that each woman had, his fear evaporated. Faith realized with disgust that he was actually *excited* to share his proclivities with them. They learned that he wasn't only spying on the victims but on many other residents throughout all three neighborhoods on his route.

"But I didn't kill anyone!" he said, "Why would I do that? How can I watch them if they're dead?"

"Poor you," Michael said drily.

"I…" the fear returned. "Please," he said, "You have to believe me!"

Faith watched him closely. No twitch. No swallow. She looked at Turk and Turk reluctantly sat back on his heels and stopped growling at Fenimore.

Dammit. She trusted Turk's intuition enough to know that Fenimore was telling the truth, but she would have to do her due diligence anyway.

"I don't have to believe you," she said. "How do I know you're telling the truth?"

"The dash cam!" he said desperately. "The mail truck has cameras. They'll show that I didn't stop long enough anywhere to bury anyone, and they'll show that I never put a body in the truck!"

"They won't show me what you did after hours."

"The apartment I live in has security cameras at the gates," he said, "You can see me going home and not leaving home every night for… God, forever. I don't really have a social life."

"Other than peeking into open windows and watching other people screw."

He hung his head and pouted in a disgusting imitation of a petulant child. "That's not the same as murder," he said softly.

"We'll check on the cameras," Faith said.

She turned to leave, Michael and Turk following.

"Hey, wait!" Fenimore said. "I'm still cuffed to the table!"

"Of course you are," Michael said. "You spied on dozens of people without their knowledge, trespassed on numerous homes, and resisted arrest. You might not be a murderer yet, Richard, but you're a grade A creep, and I don't want you anywhere near another human being for a long time."

"But… but…"

"Sergeant Anglesey will fill you in on your… rights," Michael said, lip curling in contempt. "Have a shitty day, Richard."

They left the interrogation room, ignoring Fenimore's cries of protest as they met Anglesey. They conferred briefly with him, then talked a uniform into giving them a ride back to their vehicle.

They reached the diner and waved a farewell to the uniform just before Faith's cell phone rang. It was the Boss.

"Hi Boss," she said.

"You want to tell me what the hell is going on?" the Boss said. "You have three victims and more suspects than I can count, and not *one* of them is an actual lead?"

"I'm sorry, Boss," Faith said.

"Sorry? For fuck's sake, Bold, I have the Deputy Director and the DA breathing down my neck, and you're *sorry?"*

"We're doing our best, sir," Faith said.

"Well, your best is shit," the Boss said. "And it better not be your best. You two are supposed to be my finest investigators, and so far I have nothing but a bunch of running around in circles."

Faith took a breath and tried to keep her voice steady. "It always seems that way, sir, but we're not running in circles. We're—"

"Oh, that's right," the Boss said, "you're just fucking everything up. You didn't think to follow up with the HOA for days, you didn't think to widen your net to include contractors until just now, and you've run yourself ragged interrogating people instead of doing any kind of investigative work that might narrow your suspect pool."

Faith's jaw tightened again, and she felt heat creep up her cheeks. The Boss was right. That was the worst part. He was right, and Faith herself had noticed the lapses in judgment both she and Michael had shown. At the same time, even if they had been right on top of everything, they wouldn't be any farther along than they were now. None of their leads had panned out, and they still didn't have a clue who their murderer was.

"Sir, I understand that this is frustrating," she said, keeping her tone even, "but we're doing everything we can. This killer knows Cedar Hills very well and is incredibly skilled at covering his tracks."

"Skilled?" the Boss shouted. "He practically handed you the third victim. Christ, Bold, he buried her in the *first victim's backyard!*"

Faith didn't say anything. She didn't know what else to say.

"You need to be honest with me, Bold. Is your PTSD affecting your ability to do your job?"

Faith stiffened. “No, sir,” she said brittlely.

“You’d better not be lying to me,” he said. “If you need time off and therapy, I’m good with that. If you’re ignoring the warning signs and endangering people because you’re too fucking stubborn to admit that you need help, then we’re going to have a problem. A career-ending problem. Are we clear, Bold?”

“Crystal,” Faith replied.

“We better be.”

The Boss hung up, and Faith sighed and lowered her phone, but just then it rang again. This time, it was Laszlo Kovacs.

“Special Agent Prince,” he said imperiously.

“This is Bold,” Faith replied.

“In my twenty years of residence in this community,” Kovacs continued, ignoring Faith, “I have never been witness to such a travesty of justice as this. Your job, Special Agent, is to apprehend the fiend who has been terrorizing the good people of Cedar Hills, and what do you have to show for it?”

“Mr. Kovacs,” Faith said, pressing her fingers to her temples. “I assure you, the police, the sheriff’s department and the FBI are all working diligently to ensure—”

“Save your excuses for the press conference, Special Agent,” Kovacs interrupted. “Even now, I have the distinguished representatives of the press in my office demanding answers. What shall I tell them, Special Agent?”

“Wait,” Faith said, “You have reporters in your office right now?”

“Of course,” Kovacs said, “They demand to know—”

Faith hung up and pressed both hands to the sides of her head, breathing deeply to keep from screaming in frustration. Maybe the Boss and Kovacs would like to relieve her and Michael. No doubt they would quickly put an end to things and ride off into the sunset on the backs of loud, raucous cheers from the grateful populace.

“It was only a matter of time before we ran into the press,” Michael said. “Frankly, I’m amazed that we made it as long as we did without dodging questions from reporters.”

“The Boss probably ran interference for us,” Faith said, lowering her hands. “And now he can’t anymore, which is why he’s pissed. This makes everyone involved look bad, and Cedar Hills is full of people who are desperate not to look bad.”

“Including the DA’s uncle,” Michael said. “We sure he’s not involved?”

Faith laughed mirthlessly. “He hasn’t even been in town since the murders started. Left three days before Somersall bit it. He goes on vacation to Paris every summer.”

“Wait,” Michael said. “He’s not even in town?”

“Nope,” Faith said, “I imagine the DA’s hoping this is old news by the time he returns. Can’t have the family name besmirched by all of this.”

“Christ,” Michael said. “The shittiest of shit shows.”

Faith sighed. “I need some air,” she said. “You take Turk back to the hotel. I’ll walk. Maybe I’ll get lucky and something will fall into place in my head.”

“Suit yourself,” Michael said, “but it’s three miles back to the hotel.”

“I can walk three miles,” Faith said. “I just need some space.”

“Sure thing,” he said.

Turk barked and planted his feet, glaring stubbornly at Michael when he called him to the car.

“Go ahead, boy,” Faith said. “I’ll just be a few minutes behind you.”

Turk whined and barked at Michael when Michael called him again.

“It’s okay,” Faith insisted. “I’ll be fine, boy.”

Turk whined once more, then reluctantly allowed Michael to lead him away. Faith smiled at him, then started off. A moment later, the SUV passed her, and she waved as it accelerated down the road toward the hotel.

***

Faith walked, but not toward the hotel. She couldn’t shake the feeling that she was missing something, something important that if she could only understand would reveal everything she needed to know about the case and lead them to the killer. She had no idea what that thing might be.

“It’s supposed to be different,” she said out loud.

Nope. Still no idea what was supposed to be different.

“We need to make fuel injectors, not carburetors,” she said.

Nope. Their first fuel injector was a failure.

“Goddammit,” she said.

God, as usual, had nothing to say.

She walked, not entirely sure where she was going until she looked up and saw a beautifully engraved marble sign that read Welcome to Cedar Hills in unnecessarily flowery script.

"All roads lead to Rome," she muttered under her breath.

She walked through the perfectly manicured footpaths and gleaming streets, wondering how many taxpayer dollars went to ensuring that not a single leaf or a speck of dust remained on the asphalt or concrete. Maybe the HOA dues covered that. Faith had glanced at the monthly dues and they were exorbitant, to say the least.

She walked for a solid hour before realizing where she was headed. The street sign read Rosewood Place. A quarter-mile ahead lay 16805 Rosewood Place, the Gonzalez residence.

Faith wasn't entirely sure what she was looking for, but her best intuitions typically came from allowing herself to wander. She walked to the door and knocked. There was no answer. She tried again, but still no answer.

Faith hesitated, but only briefly. She removed her hairpin, and stuck it into the knob, carefully working it through the lock until the latch clicked and the handle turned. She walked inside, carefully closing and locking the door behind her.

"Mr. Gonzalez?" she called. "Dom?"

No answer. She saw a laptop on the table and opened it. It was password protected. She had a tool to crack computers, but it was at the hotel, so she left it.

She decided Dom must have left to visit family, or possibly to make arrangements for his wife. She hoped to be out of here before he returned, but if she wasn't she could easily explain herself by saying she was looking for clues for his wife's murder, which is exactly what she was doing.

She saw a sheaf of papers on the kitchen counter and began leafing through them. The top paper was a note that read, 4:40pm Chicago, Julio. An arrival time, a destination, and the name Carlos would probably be Carlos Rosas, Ariana's brother. That explained Dom's whereabouts.

The other papers were harder to determine. There were plans to remodel their kitchen with granite countertops and stainless steel smart appliances. There were brochures for vacations to five-star resorts in such fanciful destinations as Bali, Puerto Vallarta, Rio de Janeiro, and the ever-ubiquitous Maui.

Faith frowned. The Gonzalezs must be well off to afford living in Cedar Hills, but they would have to be doing very well to afford all of this.

Then again, Ariana was apparently quite good at pleasing Hector, and Hector seemed to be doing better than Dom was. Maybe he was planning a little getaway for the two of them, and maybe Ariana was showing some of the skills to which Fenimore alluded to earn herself a new kitchen.

She headed upstairs to their bedroom. The bed was unmade, and the room disheveled. Women's clothing lay scattered everywhere, and Faith knew the room hadn't been touched since Ariana died. She thought it would be a while before Dom ever entered the room again.

She saw another laptop on the small desk in the room. She doubted this one would be unlocked but tried it anyway.

The screen immediately came to life, and asked Faith for no password, pin, or facial recognition. She tapped the mouse and the laptop opened to a smiling picture of a younger, thinner, and happier Dom with a young Ariana smiling and riding piggyback at a beach that Faith didn't recognize but was almost certainly not any of the exotic locales to where Ariana intended to vacation with her new beau.

She opened the internet browser and checked Ariana's emails. Most of them were innocuous. There was the usual sea of spam and ads, a few emails from the church and several from Hector. Faith chuckled when she saw the explicit messages and pictures the two emailed back and forth. She wondered if Ariana ever thought of the irony of having a picture of her with her husband as a screensaver on the laptop she used to send nudes to the man she was cuckolding him with. She doubted it. Like most cheaters, she was probably too concerned with herself to think about anyone else.

She checked Ariana's internet history and found a screen full of links to various shopping websites. She opened a few and her eyes widened appreciatively. Ariana had expensive tastes. A few of the websites were for luxury vehicles. Real luxury vehicles, not the cheap Audis and BMWs that people bought when they couldn't afford the high end models.

She had scheduled an appointment with a representative from Bentley USA to discuss a model that retailed for over three hundred thousand dollars. Not even Hector had that kind of money, unless he had skeletons that Faith hadn't uncovered yet.

A thought occurred to Faith. Maybe Ariana was the one with another skeleton.

She closed the laptop and headed downstairs and outside, locking the door on her way out. She called Michael and when he answered, said, “Hey, come pick me up. I’m at the Gonzalez place.”

Michael sighed. “How did I know you were going to call me to come get you?”

“Quit whining,” she said. “I have another lead.”

“Oh joy,” he said drily. “No doubt this will finally be the one that breaks the case.”

“If it is, you owe me a very expensive dinner,” Faith said. “See you soon.”

CHAPTER EIGHTEEN

"Wow," Michael said, "what a peach she was."

"Another shining example of community," Faith agreed.

"Shall we go talk to the lawyer and confirm our suspicions?" Michael said.

"It's only right," she agreed.

An hour or so of digging uncovered a sudden and drastic increase in Ariana Gonzalez's personal fortune. A few more minutes of digging revealed that this increase coincided suspiciously with the passing of Mrs. Gonzalez's grandfather and the shunting of her grandmother to a nursing home that was the polar opposite of upscale. Neither of them wanted to suggest that Ariana had murdered her grandfather for money, but neither of them would be surprised to find out that was the case.

They reached the law offices of Hammersmith and Weiss ten minutes later. The way the case was going so far, Faith was surprised that Porter & Somersall weren't representing Mrs. Gonzalez.

They caught Eric Weiss just as he was locking up his office for the day. He took one look at the agents and went white.

"Good afternoon, Mr. Weiss," Faith said. "Got a minute?"

He sighed. "I doubt I have a choice," he said.

"Smart guy," Michael deadpanned. "You should be a lawyer."

"I'm assuming you're police?" Mr. Weiss said.

"FBI," Faith replied. "Would you like to see our IDs?"

"You know I have to," Weiss asked, resigned.

Faith and Michael showed Weiss their laminates. Weiss nodded and asked, "Does the dog have to join us?"

"Special Agent Turk is a valuable member of the Bureau and a key part of this investigation," Faith replied. "I value his instincts."

Weiss shrugged. "All right. I guess it won't make a difference."

He led them into the office and offered them a seat. When the two agents sat, he sat behind the desk and said, "All right, let's get this over with."

"Sounds like you already know why we're here," Faith said, "so I'll cut right to the chase. When did Mr. Rosas change his will to leave everything to Ariana?"

"I can't tell you that," Weiss said. "It's protected by lawyer-client confidentiality."

"Not anymore," Michael said. "Mrs. Gonzalez is dead, as is Mr. Rosas. If you'd prefer, we can get a warrant, but maybe that will raise too many eyebrows. On that note, how is Mr. Hammersmith? Do you think he'd be more forthcoming?"

At the mention of his partner's name, Weiss paled. "No, no, that's all right. It—look, agents, I did nothing wrong. I did my job as required—"

"I'll be honest with you, Mr. Weiss," Faith interrupted. "I couldn't care less. Tell me right now what happened with Mr. Rosas's will, and I'll keep not caring. Stall anymore, and I'll start caring enough to call the bar, Judge Garland, and Mr. Hammersmith and let them know that a certain Mr. Weiss accepted a rather large paycheck for the execution of Ramon Rosas's will and that the sole beneficiary of that will—your client—was mysteriously murdered less than a month after receiving the settlement."

"Okay, okay," he said. He ran his hands through thinning hair and said. "Look, you have to promise not to tell anyone."

"We don't have to promise shit," Faith said, "But I *do* promise that my one goal in life will be to ruin you as publicly as possible if you don't start talking."

Weiss heaved a sigh. "All right," he said. He heaved another sigh, then said, "Ramon Rosas was ninety years old when he died. For the eight years before his death, he was slowly but surely slipping into dementia. By the time he died, there were still occasional lucid days, but they were few and far between."

"Two months ago, Mrs. Gonzalez came to me with a new will. She claimed it was revised by her grandfather just before he was placed into hospice. She claimed it was during a lucid moment that he changed the will to leave everything to her. It had his signature, and the two witnesses required by law."

"And you weren't present to sign," Faith added.

Weiss slumped further in his chair. "No."

"But you signed it anyway."

"Yes."

"Even though you knew it was bullshit."

"Hey, I didn't know it was bullshit," Weiss protested. "For all I know, it could have been valid. Mr. Rosas *did* have moments of lucidity, right up until his death."

"Don't feed us that line," Michael said. "Even if he had moments of lucidity, no lawyer in their right mind would have considered him of sound enough mind to sign a will. Unless, of course, that lawyer was of a mind to receive a very substantial stipend for his services as executor."

Weiss remained silent.

"You're smart enough to know that silence only buys you time," Faith said, "And you're smart enough to know I mean it when I promise you that I will put your name on every news network in Philadelphia if you—"

"Goddammit, yes," Weiss said. "Yes, I… suspected… that Mrs. Gonzalez may have taken advantage of her grandfather, but none of her relatives fought the judgment. The rest of the family was estranged from Ramon, and his wife… well, his wife was…"

"Similarly incapacitated," Michael offered.

"Yes," Weiss said.

"What did she offer you to get you to flip?" Michael asked. "Maybe a little bit of what she was spreading around town?"

Weiss scoffed. "Yes, Special Agent, it was well known that Mrs. Gonzalez was a rolling stone, but no, she didn't offer to screw me to ask no questions. Sex is nice, but money is more attractive than any woman alive when it's present in sufficient concentrations."

"So you falsified the will—" Faith began.

"I did my duty!" Weiss interrupted in what Faith was sure he thought was a thunderous voice. "It's not my place to pass judgment. If every lawyer in the country was more concerned with his own interpretation of morality than accurate representation of his clientele, then there would be no rule of law!"

"Sure," Michael said, "you keep telling yourself that."

"It's okay," Faith said. "Like I said, we're not after you."

She stood and regarded Weiss with contempt. "Thank you for your time, Mr. Weiss."

She, Turk, and Michael left the office. Weiss remained where he sat, staring ahead, and wearing a look that suggested he knew exactly how much of a low life he was.

Not that he would care for much longer. He still had his money.

***

"So we know that all of our victims had skeletons in their closet," Faith said, "and that these skeletons were serious enough that a lot of people could have had a motive to kill any one of them."

"But not all three of them," Michael said, "Because the only thing that connects all three of them is that they lived in Cedar Hills."

They were back at the hotel enjoying halfway decent Mexican food that beat the monotony of pizza and Chinese.

"So that leaves the same profile that led us to Fenimore," Faith said. "Someone who knows the neighborhood well but doesn't necessarily live there."

"True," Michael said, "but I'm thinking that our guy actually knows their secrets. All of them, not just the ones that lie on the surface. I think it's someone who hates them for their secrets. Maybe a former neighbor with a secret of his own."

"A secret the others could exploit and use to drive him out."

"Exactly," Michael said, "like Marcus Washington, but with an intact violent streak."

Faith thought of Marcus's claim that people lived in neighborhoods like these to hide. And what do cornered animals do when forced from their hiding spot? Fight or flight. Marcus, no longer wishing to be violent anymore, chose flight. Their killer had made a different choice.

"I just hate that we're jumping from profile to profile," Faith said. "Nothing's consistent. Nothing except the fact that they all live in Cedar Hills."

"So the motive has to be related to Cedar Hills," Michael said. "We've been looking at people who are either residents of the community or actively involved with it. I think we need to widen the net to include people who used to live here and have a reason to hate it and the people who live here."

"Where do we find that information?" Faith asked.

"Well," Michael said, "I have an answer, but you won't like it."

Faith stared at him for a moment, then sighed. "Dammit. All right, let's head back to the HOA office."

They reached the office ten minutes later to find Laszlo Kovacs waiting with his arms crossed like a drill instructor regarding two particularly disappointing recruits. "So once more, you two have been chasing your tails and come up with nothing. Pathetic."

"Save your judgment for the press conference," Faith retorted tartly. "We need a list of former residents that hate Cedar Hills."

"Hate Cedar Hills?" Laszlo repeated.

"Yes," Faith said, "We think the killer is targeting the neighborhood as much or more than he's targeting specific people. Do you know of anyone who might have a reason to despise the neighborhood and everyone in it?"

"Boy, you really are grasping at straws," Laszlo said.

"All right," Faith replied, turning and walking out.

"Hold on, hold on," Laszlo replied. "All right. Yes. I know of a few people. I'm sure there are more—paradise isn't for everyone—but I know of a half dozen people who hate Cedar Hills and its residents enough that they might conceivably take extreme measures. I'll draw up some names for you."

He opened his computer and began typing a document. When he finished, he clicked print and the massive dinosaur copier—an interesting relic considering how expensive everything else was here—spat out a single page.

Laszlo took the page and handed it to Faith. "I apologize for my aggressiveness," he said, "but you must understand, this is my home. I left Hungary when I was fourteen and worked very hard to be able to afford the life I now have. It's important to me that I and the others who work hard to remain here enjoy the fruits of our lifelong labors in peace and harmony. I just…" he lowered his eyes. "I feel like you and the police have seen the worst of Cedar Hills and decided that's all there is. I hope you can accept that, to most of us, this is the best we'll ever have it. I would give anything for these secrets—these murders—to disappear and for Cedar Hills to remain beautiful."

Faith tried to drum up some sympathy for Laszlo, but she couldn't. She had seen the worst of this neighborhood, and she had seen the best. The worst had run the best out of town via angry mob.

"Thank you for your time, Mr. Kovacs," she said.

Then she, Michael, and Turk left the HOA office.

They sat in the car and fired up Michael's laptop. The search was mercifully quick. Of the six names Laszlo gave them, only one of them still lived in Philadelphia.

Daniel Whitmore, fifty-three, was a former capital investment banker. He was also the leader of the HOA before Laszlo. He left the HOA, Cedar Hills, and his capital investment firm after being caught embezzling tens of millions of dollars from the company. As scandals go, his was a fairly minor one in the scheme of things, but became enough news in the local area that Whitmore had become a pariah. When the dust settled, no one in Cedar Hills wanted anything to do with him. Among those friends was Ethan Somersall, at least until Somersall decided to decline representing Mr. Whitmore.

He represented a violent woman-beater like Beau Carpenter, but Whitmore was too much for him. That, if anything, indicated how dangerous he considered Whitmore.

Daniel lost his house and all of his other assets as part of the settlement. When he finished his five-year prison sentence, the bank garnished the wages he earned as a part-time janitor at a local strip mall. According to what they were able to dig up, it would take him another nine years at those wages to pay off what he owed. In the meantime, he lived in the King Luxe Apartments on the other side of the city.

Faith glanced at her watch. Eight o'clock.

She looked at Turk, "What do you say boy? Got time for one more suspect?"

Turk barked in affirmation. Faith looked at Michael. Michael shrugged, stuffed the rest of his quesadilla in his mouth, and said, "What the hell? Worst case scenario we waste our time some more."

CHAPTER NINETEEN

The King Luxe Apartments—like most communities with such ostentatious names—was neither kingly nor luxurious. It was an ancient star-shaped agglutination of octo-plexes with plaster walls, a stucco roof, and a wrought iron fence covered in peeling, chipped, green paint.

"How the mighty fall," Michael muttered as he pulled the car to a stop in front of the complex.

"Could be worse," Faith said, thinking of the three mighty individuals who now lay buried under the ground or frozen in a morgue.

"Yeah," Michael said, "I guess you're right."

The three of them walked up to the gate. Faith buzzed the intercom, and a bored middle-aged female voice said, "Yes?"

"We're Special Agents Faith Bold and Michael Prince with our K9 unit, Turk," Faith said. "Do you have a security camera so I can show you our IDs?"

The gate buzzed and Faith heard the lock disengage. "Guess that's a no," Faith said.

"Well, it's a who cares, at least," Michael said.

The three of them walked into the complex. Whitmore was 3E, near the back of the community. They approached the unit, and Michael stood back with his hand on his firearm under his jacket while Faith knocked.

"FBI!" she called. "Daniel Whitmore? Open up!"

She heard shuffling and muttering as someone approached the door. A moment later, the door swung open and Daniel Whitmore stared sourly at the three of them. An odor of booze strong enough to make Faith's eyes water wafted from the open door.

"What do you want?" he asked.

"We're investigating a series of recent murders in the Cedar Hills community," Faith said, "We'd like to ask you a few questions."

"Fuck you," he said.

He tried to close the door, but Faith stuck her foot out and blocked it. "I'm afraid we have to insist, Mr. Whitmore."

“Well, I’m afraid you have to kiss my ass,” Whitmore said. “I don’t live there anymore, and I don’t know anything about any murders.”

“Can you tell me where you were two nights ago?” Faith asked.

“Same place I’ve been every night the past two weeks,” he said. “Damn felony convictions means I can’t even hold a job as a janitor. I’m staying here until I get evicted. Then I get to choose between a bullet and living homeless.”

Faith sighed. “Mr. Whitmore, I’m sorry for your circumstances, but I really must insist. Three people were murdered--"

"Good," he said, his voice slurring. “Fuck ‘em. Fuck ‘em all.”

“Do you have any way of proving that you were here?” Faith said. “A receipt for takeout, pay-per-view, anything?”

“No,” Daniel said.

He made to close the door again, and Faith leaned her shoulder into the door. “Mr. Whitmore, I’m going to have to ask you to come to the station with us.”

“And I’m going to have to ask you to kiss my ass!” he said again.

He lunged for Faith, shoving her backwards past the open door. Turk leapt at him, fangs bared, but Faith called him off just before Michael reached past her and pulled Whitmore bodily through the door. Whitmore struggled but when Turk growled at him, he calmed down and allowed Michael to cuff him.

They walked back to the car, dragging a protesting Whitmore with them. Whitmore’s neighbors stared impassively at them as they left the complex, their faces all betraying the same mild contempt held by all who had nothing for those who had anything.

***

“Well,” Morton said, “we’ll know for sure when he wakes up, but I think this is our guy.”

Faith looked through the two-way mirror at the sleeping form of Daniel Whitmore. He lay passed out over the table, his face resting in a slowly growing puddle of drool. Behind her, Michael and Sheriff Morton stood and watched while Turk sat in the corner wagging his tail.

After dropping Whitmore off into custody, they had quickly learned that Whitmore was in no condition to answer questions. They headed to the hotel to sleep with a promise from Morton to call them if he said anything useful.

“What makes you so sure?” Faith asked. “Did he talk at all last night?”

“Well, before he bit the dust, he ranted about how happy he was that the slut Evelyn Vance was dead, mentioned that Ethan Somersall was a snake, and opined that all Hispanic women were whores, so it made sense that Ariana Gonzalez was one too. He was ostracized by the neighborhood and lost his entire life along with it. He has an alibi that he can’t prove, and—here’s the clincher—when he passed out, I had a uniform check his hands. Dirt under every fingernail. Not dust, not grime, dirt. Like you plant flowers in.”

“That’s not enough to prove it’s him,” Michael cautioned.

“No,” Morton said, “Like I said, we’ll know more when he wakes up, hopefully at least reasonably sober.”

Faith looked back at Whitmore and said nothing. Something nagged at the back of her mind.

It made sense. Whitmore had motive, a connection to all three victims, and unlike their previous suspects, had no alibi. Turk seemed to like him as the suspect too. He spent the entire ride back to the station growling at him and snapping every time Whitmore so much as flinched.

So why couldn’t Faith accept it? Why did she feel that they once more had the wrong guy?

“It’s supposed to be different,” she said.

“What’s supposed to be different?” Morton asked.

“Nothing,” Faith said. “I’m going for a walk.”

“Everything okay?” Morton asked.

“She’s fine,” Michael said, “She gets like this sometimes. You learn to live with it.”

He grinned at Faith, but when Faith didn’t offer a snappy retort or an upraised middle finger in response, his grin vanished. “That being said, *are* you okay?”

“I’m all right,” she said. “I just need to clear my head.”

“At least take Turk this time,” Michael said. “He gets anxious when you’re more than three feet away from him.”

Turk barked hurtfully at Michael and Michael chuckled. “It’s okay, man, I used to feel the same way. You’ll grow out of it.”

This time, Faith did offer him a finger, but she also called Turk to follow her. They walked to a community park a quarter-mile from the station. Turk flitted from bush to bush, sniffing and wagging his tail.

He was nearly seven years old but still acted like a puppy when not actively working on a case.

Faith watched him play and sifted through the thoughts tumbling through her mind.

It's supposed to be different. That was the key. That was the phrase that, if understood, would lead Faith to the answer. But what was supposed to be different?

The neighborhood, of course. Cedar Hills was supposed to be different. Cedar Hills was supposed to be different, but Daniel didn't want it to be different. He just hated it. He couldn't care less if it changed or remained the same. He wanted the people there to hurt, and he didn't care about much else.

The other suspects all wanted their own circumstances to be different. So did the victims. They wanted a new spouse, a new kitchen, more success in their field, all things related only to themselves and not the neighborhood as a whole. Their families didn't want anything to be different. They wanted to insist that nothing was different, that the beautiful dream they were living was real and nothing existed to challenge that reality.

Even Laszlo didn't want things to be different. He didn't even care that the reality of Cedar Hills was evil and crime-ridden. He just didn't want anyone to know about the dirt.

Faith fixated on that point. The dirt. Dirt under Daniel's fingernails. Dirt on the residents of Cedar Hills. Dirt under which bodies were buried.

Dirt like the dirt that Turk was now digging.

"Whatcha got there boy?" she asked.

He came up, wagging his tail and happily biting down on a squeaky toy that some other dog had buried. He dropped the toy and held it down with his paw, working happily at it and making little snuffing noises of contentment.

Dogs didn't bury things because they hated them. They buried things because they wanted to hide them from others.

Do you know why people live in neighborhoods like this, Miss Bold? They live here to hide.

And sometimes they don't hide very well. Sometimes, they have to be hidden.

It's supposed to be different.

Then it all made sense.

"Turk, come!" Faith called, sprinting to the road.

Turk instantly dropped the toy and followed after her.

As she ran, Faith lifted her phone to call for a car, but saw a cab and flagged that down instead. She gave the driver the address to the HOA office of the Cedar Hills neighborhood. She checked her phone on the way. Nine-thirty. Good. Laszlo would still be in.

She debated calling Michael but decided to leave him to question Whitmore until she was sure she was onto something helpful. This time though, she thought she had the answer.

"There's an extra twenty in it if you get there in ten minutes," Faith told the driver.

The driver dutifully hit the gas and the ancient sedan surged forward. Faith felt her heart start to beat faster, and a small smile played at the corners of her lips.

"We got him, boy," she whispered to Turk. "This time, we got him."

CHAPTER TWENTY

He hated being angry. It was an ugly emotion. There was no point to it. It wasn't productive to be angry. You didn't shout obscenities at a weed; you pulled it. You didn't argue with deviants, you buried them before their deviance could spread, before the beautiful neighborhood you finally found, the one free of the selfish, gluttonous, greedy, vain fools who made this world such an incredible cesspool, turned into yet another pile of filth.

But these… these FBI agents had ruined everything. No, not the agents. It was that storm. That damned storm and that meddlesome Andrew Milton.

He shut off the tv and stared at the blank screen, breathing slowly in through his nose and out through his mouth. His hands tensed and relaxed rhythmically as he tried to calm himself.

He had thought for sure that burying Evelyn Vance in their garden was safe. After all, that fence had stood for years and survived countless storms.

But as he knew very well, it only took one weed to ruin an entire garden.

Of course, that second weed sprouted the same day the first weed did. He couldn't forget that the one body he had buried in a public place was found on the same day as Evelyn.

Breathe in. Hold. Breathe out.

And now the agents were making things worse. He had buried Ariana Gonzalez at the Somersall residence thinking that they would never suspect the killer to be that brazen. Then the dog had somehow smelled and unearthed her.

And now his neighborhood—his beautiful, perfect Cedar Hills—was plastered all over the news with taglines such as Neighborhood from Hell, Nightmare in Cedar Hills, and Are Your Neighbors Watching? Thanks to some overzealous federal agents who shouldn't even be on this case, his garden was revealed to be full of weeds, and he couldn't even come forward to reassure everyone that he was handling it, it would be okay, he would pull the weeds, and everything would be fine.

Didn't I tell you, Horace? Carmen's nasal drone sounded in his mind. *Didn't I tell you that if you keep meddling, it will come back to bite you someday?*

"Shut up, Carmen," he said softly. "You never went a day in your life without meddling."

Carmen was the first weed he'd pulled. He tried for years to get her to stop gossiping and spreading rumors, but she never did. He tolerated it as much as he could, but when her rumors began to spread throughout Cedar Hills—his perfect garden—and she still wouldn't keep her mouth shut, he had finally realized he needed to take matters into his own hands.

So, he had pulled his first weed, stifling it in its sleep, and using the body to fertilize his harlequin blue flag irises.

He had pulled four more weeds and planted their bodies in his yard. When he had run out of room in his own garden, he had moved on to his neighbors' gardens. Seven more weeds were pulled before Ethan Somersall.

Twelve times. Twelve times he had been successful, and then the bottom had fallen out.

Breathe in. Hold. Breathe out.

He should stop. He realized that now. He should stop before he went too far. The wasps were watching now. They didn't like that he was pulling weeds. They were waiting to sting him—to stop him so the weeds could take over the garden and the flowers and bees were choked off and driven away.

He needed to wait, to lay low until this case faded into the background, and he could work unseen again.

He needed to stop, but he couldn't. If he waited too long, the weeds would take over, and it would be too late.

He stood and stretched, breathing in deeply one final time, holding it, then breathing out. He picked up his hat, settled it on his head, grabbed his sap, and got to work.

***

Beau Carpenter answered the door, wearing his trademark smile. He regarded Beau's figure—youthful and strong despite being no more than ten years younger than he was. He respected Beau's physique. It was difficult to maintain a body like his into one's forties. He should know.

“Can I help you?” Beau asked.

He almost wished he didn’t have to pull this weed. On the outside, Beau was a perfect specimen. He was beautiful.

But then, nightshades were beautiful. Beautiful, fast-spreading, and entirely poisonous.

“Good evening, Mr. Carpenter,” Horace said softly. “Are you sleeping with Candace DeGroot, Millicent Towney, and Carolyn Saint-Pierre?

Beau’s smile vanished. “Who the fuck are you? You’re not Jacques Saint-Pierre. Are you Gavin DeGroot? Jamal Towney? No, you don’t look like a Jamal. You must be Gavin. Well, look man, sorry about it, but she came onto me, you know what I mean?”

“It doesn’t matter,” Horace said without raising his voice. “You could have declined her advances. Everyone has a choice.”

“Yeah, well I chose to fuck your wife better than you ever could,” Beau sneered. “Now get the fuck off my porch.”

Horace sighed. “Well, I tried.”

“Yeah?” Beau said. “Try this.”

He threw a lighting fast right hook aimed squarely at Horace’s jaw. Horace, however, saw it coming and easily bobbed under the punch. On the weave, he pulled his hand from behind his back and brought it down heavily on Beau’s head. Beau sighed softly, then went limp.

Horace caught him just before he hit the ground and with a grunt of effort, lifted the man over his shoulders and carried him to his waiting car.

This time, he would bury the weed somewhere it would never be found.

CHAPTER TWENTY ONE

Faith barged into the HOA office, surprising Laszlo Kovacs and an elderly woman Faith guessed was another member of the board.

"I have a new profile," Faith began immediately. "Someone who lives alone. Someone who's lived here a long time, probably decades. Someone who knows people but is probably not closely involved with anyone. Someone reclusive and physically strong enough to overpower a healthy adult and bury them himself."

Laszlo blinked. "Well, I would say Beau Carpenter, but I understand you've already ruled him out."

"Anyone else?" Faith said, "Anyone at all?"

"Well," the older woman began.

Faith whirled on her. The older woman blinked and said, "Well, you might try Horace Greenwood. He's lived alone ever since his wife died. Near sixty I'd guess, but still in good shape. Used to be a boxer in his day. Just gardens now."

"Give me his address," Faith said. "Quickly."

"All right," Laszlo said, "I'll look it up. Are you sure it's him?"

"As sure as I am of anything," Faith said.

"Well," Laszlo replied, handing Faith a paper with the address written down, "good luck, Special Agent."

"Thank you," Faith said. "Before I leave, Mr. Laszlo, let me make it clear how critical it is that this information not leave this room. We can't have another incident like the mob at Mr. Washington's house."

"I understand," Kovacs said. "I won't say anything."

Faith looked at the older woman sitting next to Laszlo. She shook her head in acknowledgment and Faith said, "Good. Turk, come."

The two of them rushed out of the office and began to sprint toward the address. After a hundred yards, Faith slowed to a jog. It wouldn't do for her to be winded when she confronted him, especially if he was a former boxer still powerful enough to incapacitate an adult male. She knew how dangerous it could be to confront someone like that on her own.

As she jogged, she called Michael. When he answered, she said, "Michael, it's Faith. Whitmore's not the guy. I'm going to text you an address. Get here as soon as possible and bring the cavalry."

"Jeez, Faith," Michael said, "can I convince you to wait for us?"

"No,"

Michael sighed. "All right. Give me the address."

"1684 Peony Way."

"Roger that. We're fifteen minutes out."

"Make it ten," Faith said, rounding the corner onto Peony Way.

She hung up and slowed to a walk the last fifty yards to the house, looking around for any sign of activity. There was none, and when she knocked repeatedly on the door, there was no answer. She drew her weapon and prepared to break the door, but stopped when Turk pricked his ears.

"Got something, boy?" she asked.

Turk barked affirmation, then launched off behind the house. Faith followed at a dead run, giving up on saving her energy as she struggled to keep up with the excited dog. Turk led her through the footpaths and cul-de-sacs and community parks of Cedar Hills to a new development near Peony Lane.

He sprinted to one of the new houses, so new that the front yard hadn't yet been seeded. He leapt the fence to the backyard.

"Turk, wait!" Faith called, vaulting the fence behind him.

And coming face to face with Horace Greenwood.

Horace looked at Faith in shock, and Faith had enough time to realize that Horace was in phenomenal shape for a man his age, hell, any age. His abs rippled and his chest bulged under his tight shirt and the muscles in the arms that held the shovel he was using to bury the body lying on the ground next to him were taut and defined.

Faith's eyes fell to the body and widened when she recognized it as that of Beau Carpenter.

Turk barked suddenly and leapt toward Horace. Faith lifted her eyes just in time to see the shovel aimed—blade first—at her skull. She jumped back with a cry and the blade whistled just in front of her nose, right before Turk sank his teeth into Horace's arm.

Instead of the cry she expected, Horace grimaced in a look that communicated more annoyance than pain. With a mighty swing of his arm, he sent Turk tumbling away.

Faith regained her feet and rushed Horace. He swung the shovel again and Faith ducked under it and landed a kick to Horace's ankles.

He stumbled and as Faith stood, she landed an elbow flush to his temple. He staggered back, blinking, and Faith grabbed the shovel and yanked.

The handle slid through Horace's hands, but before it could slide out, he grabbed the end and pulled back. The motion seemed unsteady and almost accidental but still managed to pull Faith nearly off of her feet.

God, he was strong.

Turk leapt at him again, but this time Horace was ready. He released the shovel, drove his fist into the side of Turk's head, sending the dog sprawling, and reached across his body with the other hand to grab the shovel before Faith could steady herself.

He swung backhand with both hands. Faith tried to hold onto the shovel, but the centrifugal force lifted her off of her feet and tore the handle from her grasp. She stumbled backward and stepped into the hole Horace was digging for Beau's body.

Faith's ankle twisted sharply, and she cried out as pain shot through her leg. Horace approached with frightening speed, but then Turk was in between them, teeth bared, dancing out of the way of Horace's swings and rushing him every time he tried to approach Faith.

Faith called to Turk and jerked her head to the left. Turk turned to Horace, feigned a rush, then leapt to the left.

Sensing an opening, Horace rushed Faith. She lunged forward, diving under the swinging shovel just before it crashed to the ground where her head was a moment ago.

Faith's ankle screamed in pain, drawing an audible cry from her as she forced herself to her knees. Horace turned and lunged again.

This was it. She didn't have room in the tank for more. If she didn't take him down now, she would end up spending eternity next to Beau Carpenter.

She gathered her strength, and with a cry, drove herself forward and wrapped her arms around his ankles, taking him to the ground. She looked up to see Turk grabbing Horace's arms and holding him down. Horace stiffened, preparing to fight them off, but just then Faith heard sirens and a moment later, Michael and half a dozen uniformed officers rushed into the backyard.

Faith rolled off of Horace, breathing heavily. Michael holstered his weapon and offered her a hand. Faith grimaced and lifted her injured ankle, holding onto Michael for support.

"Well," Michael said, "You look better than last time."

Faith laughed and rolled her eyes. "Thanks for that."
"Anytime," Michael said.
He looked at Beau and said, "Holy Christ, he's still alive."
Faith looked at Beau's prostrate body, and saw the man groaning and lifting a trembling hand to his swollen head. "So he is," she said. "I guess that counts as a victory."
"I'll take it," Michael said.

***

Faith and Michael stared in shock as Cantor wheeled yet another body from Horace's backyard. "That's the last one," he said to the two of them. "Here, at least."
"Is he talking yet?" Michael asked.
"Oh yeah," Cantor said, "singing like a canary. From what I understand, he's been very cooperative and very docile."
"So was Ed Gein," Michael said.
"Hey, I'm not defending him," Cantor said. "I'm just grateful he's not causing trouble. You saw him; he looks like Tyson's white doppelganger."
"Good thing he doesn't fight like Tyson," Michael opined.
Faith said nothing. She was thinking about what would have happened if Turk hadn't been there.
Cantor waved a goodbye then moved on with the last of the bodies. They were mostly skeletons now, and a positive identification wouldn't be possible for most of them. Faith wondered how many more they would find, then decided she didn't want to know. Their work here was done. She was looking forward to leaving Cedar Hills for good.
"What do you say we get out of here and never come back?" Michael asked.
"Fine with me," she said.
"Stop for coffee on the way back?" Michael asked.
"As long as you don't mind having it at the station," Faith said.
"What?" Michael asked. "The station? Why?"
"I want to talk to him," she said. "I need to know why."
Michael looked as though he was about to protest, but he knew her well enough to know such an effort was pointless. So, he just nodded and helped Faith to the car, Turk walking protectively next to them.

***

Horace sat in the same room where Beau Carpenter and Daniel Whitmore once sat. Faith noticed that the shackles they used for Horace's hands were heavier than the ones used for the other two.

He smiled when Faith walked in, limping slightly, and sat in front of him. "I'm sorry for your injury," he said. "I hope it's nothing permanent."

His voice was soft and gentle, utterly incongruous with his powerful body. The sentiment wasn't especially surprising to Faith. A lot of killers were polite to a fault, even to people they had recently tried to kill.

"Should be right as rain in a few days," she said, "Can't say the same for Beau Carpenter."

"Is he dead then?" Horace asked hopefully.

"No," Faith said, "but he'll be lucky if he doesn't spend the rest of his life drinking through a straw."

"Ah," Horace said, "Well, I suppose that's good enough."

"Why?" Faith asked. "Why did you do it?"

Horace smiled slightly. "I don't think my answer will satisfy you, Special Agent."

"Try me."

He sighed. "Gardening is hard work, Special Agent. Nature is beautiful, but it is also fragile. It takes care and love to keep a garden healthy, and one must always be on the lookout for weeds."

"Weeds, Special Agent, grow quickly and their roots grow deep. They spread fast and leech the life from the soil, killing the fragile, beautiful garden and leaving something ugly and twisted in their wake. The only way to stop an infestation of weeds is to pull them out, roots and all."

"So these people were weeds."

"You knew them as well as I, Special Agent. You tell me."

Faith watched Horace silently for a moment, then stood. She found she had nothing more to say to him.

"I said you wouldn't like my answer, Special Agent," Horace said.

Faith didn't reply. When she reached the car, Michael asked, "Had enough?"

"Yes," she said. "More than enough. Let's go home."

The car pulled smoothly out of the station and accelerated toward the city. Behind them, a beautiful neighborhood with manicured lawns and meticulous landscaping rapidly began the process of burying their secrets once more. It wouldn't do to have people think that Cedar Hills was as evil and violent as the world outside.

After all, Cedar Hills was supposed to be different.

EPILOGUE

"And you don't think you deserved a medal for that?" David asked incredulously.

Faith shrugged. "I mean, stuff like that happens all the time. The only ones who get medals are the ones who happen to be seen by brass or reporters. Or the ones who die. In my case, it was brass."

"I'll accept that other people deserve medals and don't get them," David said, "but I won't accept that you don't deserve one yourself."

Faith smiled at him. "Well, thank you. I appreciate that."

David laughed, and Faith thought it might be the most beautiful sound she had ever heard.

It wasn't just his breathtaking looks, though. He was sweet and kind and down-to-earth in a way that very few handsome young men were. He seemed to genuinely care for his patients, and he seemed genuinely interested in Faith.

She trusted him, too. Far more than she had trusted anyone else. It was strange and a little scary, but it felt good to trust someone enough to share the secret parts of her life with. She hadn't talked to anyone about the war. Not even Michael.

She decided that would be as far as the sharing went for tonight, though. She liked David and hoped that she could soon feel completely at ease with how comfortable she felt with him, but their relationship was still new. They were at the start of their journey together, and she would enjoy every step.

The date proceeded in a similar fashion. They didn't end up sleeping with each other that night, but when David dropped her off at her apartment, he asked if she might be available for dinner again the following weekend.

Faith smiled and said, "I might."

Then she kissed him.

It was a short kiss and just sensual enough not to be chaste, but it warmed Faith from head to toe, and when she pulled away, her lips tingled from the contact.

"Wow," David said softly.

Faith giggled. "I'll see you later, Dr. Friedman."

"See you later, Special Agent Bold."

She giggled again, offered him a final kiss on his cheek, then walked inside.

Turk barked a greeting and approached her, wagging his tail.

Faith smiled and bent over to ruffle his fur. "Well boy," she said, "I might be in love."

***

She swooned over David for a solid hour, but as the tingling in her lips faded, another pressing concern filled her mind. She pulled the files she had retrieved from the bottom of the filing cabinet in her office and began to look through them.

Most of the information was stuff she already knew or suspected, but there was one name that stood out.

Greenwood. Jared Greenwood.

Greenwood.

Faith's brow furrowed. She opened her laptop and searched for Jared Greenwood.

She found it on the third page of the results. It was an old article from a sports magazine that was maybe thirty years old. The headline read WELTERWEIGHT PHENOM HORACE GREENWOOD DIVORCES WIFE AFTER SHOCKING RETIREMENT ANNOUNCEMENT.

The article named the wife as Imogene, nee Clark, and the six-year-old son the couple shared as Jared.

Her eyes widened. So Horace—the Weed Killer—had a son connected to the copycat Donkey Killer case.

"It's supposed to be different," she whispered.

But then, it never is.

NOW AVAILABLE!

SO SCARED
(A Faith Bold Mystery—Book 3)

A new serial killer leaves a mysterious signature—the theft of his victims' wedding rings—and as the trail grows cold, FBI Special Agent Faith Bold knows she will be unable to solve it without the expert assistance of her K9 German Shepherd, Turk. But Faith still suffers from PTSD, haunted by her encounter with a serial killer, and it is only Turk who keeps her going. Together, they will stop at nothing to bring the next killer to justice—and to save the next victim before it is too late.

"A masterpiece of thriller and mystery."
—Books and Movie Reviews, Roberto Mattos (re Once Gone)

SO SCARED is Book #3 in a long-anticipated new series by #1 bestseller and USA Today bestselling author Blake Pierce, whose bestseller Once Gone (a free download) has received over 7,000 five star ratings and reviews.

FBI Special Agent Faith Bold doesn't believe she can ever return to the force after the trauma she's been through. Suffering from past demons, she feels unfit for duty and content to retire—until Turk walks into her life.

Turk, a former Marine Corps dog, wounded in battle, suffers from his own demons. But he never lets it show as he gives everything to Faith to get her back on her feet.

Each are slow to warm up to each other, but when they do, they are inseparable. Each is equally determined to hunt down the demons chasing them, whatever the cost, and to watch each other's backs—even at the risk of their own life.

A page-turning and harrowing crime thriller featuring a brilliant and tortured FBI agent, the Faith Bold series is a riveting mystery, packed with non-stop action, suspense, twists and turns, revelations, and driven by a breakneck pace that will keep you flipping pages late into the night. Fans of Rachel Caine, Teresa Driscoll and Robert Dugoni are sure to fall in love.

Future books in the series are now also available.

“An edge of your seat thriller in a new series that keeps you turning pages! ...So many twists, turns and red herrings… I can't wait to see what happens next.”
—Reader review (Her Last Wish)

“A strong, complex story about two FBI agents trying to stop a serial killer. If you want an author to capture your attention and have you guessing, yet trying to put the pieces together, Pierce is your author!”
—Reader review (Her Last Wish)

“A typical Blake Pierce twisting, turning, roller coaster ride suspense thriller. Will have you turning the pages to the last sentence of the last chapter!!!”
—Reader review (City of Prey)

“Right from the start we have an unusual protagonist that I haven't seen done in this genre before. The action is nonstop… A very atmospheric novel that will keep you turning pages well into the wee hours.”
—Reader review (City of Prey)

“Everything that I look for in a book… a great plot, interesting characters, and grabs your interest right away. The book moves along at a breakneck pace and stays that way until the end. Now on go I to book two!”
—Reader review (Girl, Alone)

“Exciting, heart pounding, edge of your seat book… a must read for mystery and suspense readers!”
—Reader review (Girl, Alone)

Blake Pierce

Blake Pierce is the USA Today bestselling author of the RILEY PAGE mystery series, which includes seventeen books. Blake Pierce is also the author of the MACKENZIE WHITE mystery series, comprising fourteen books; of the AVERY BLACK mystery series, comprising six books; of the KERI LOCKE mystery series, comprising five books; of the MAKING OF RILEY PAIGE mystery series, comprising six books; of the KATE WISE mystery series, comprising seven books; of the CHLOE FINE psychological suspense mystery, comprising six books; of the JESSIE HUNT psychological suspense thriller series, comprising twenty-eight books; of the AU PAIR psychological suspense thriller series, comprising three books; of the ZOE PRIME mystery series, comprising six books; of the ADELE SHARP mystery series, comprising sixteen books, of the EUROPEAN VOYAGE cozy mystery series, comprising six books; of the LAURA FROST FBI suspense thriller, comprising eleven books; of the ELLA DARK FBI suspense thriller, comprising fourteen books (and counting); of the A YEAR IN EUROPE cozy mystery series, comprising nine books, of the AVA GOLD mystery series, comprising six books; of the RACHEL GIFT mystery series, comprising ten books (and counting); of the VALERIE LAW mystery series, comprising nine books (and counting); of the PAIGE KING mystery series, comprising eight books (and counting); of the MAY MOORE mystery series, comprising eleven books; of the CORA SHIELDS mystery series, comprising eight books (and counting); of the NICKY LYONS mystery series, comprising eight books (and counting), of the CAMI LARK mystery series, comprising eight books (and counting), of the AMBER YOUNG mystery series, comprising five books (and counting), of the DAISY FORTUNE mystery series, comprising five books (and counting), of the FIONA RED mystery series, comprising five books (and counting), and of the new FAITH BOLD mystery series, comprising five books (and counting).

An avid reader and lifelong fan of the mystery and thriller genres, Blake loves to hear from you, so please feel free to visit www.blakepierceauthor.com to learn more and stay in touch.

BOOKS BY BLAKE PIERCE

FAITH BOLD MYSTERY SERIES
SO LONG (Book #1)
SO COLD (Book #2)
SO SCARED (Book #3)
SO NORMAL (Book #4)
SO FAR GONE (Book #5)

FIONA RED MYSTERY SERIES
LET HER GO (Book #1)
LET HER BE (Book #2)
LET HER HOPE (Book #3)
LET HER WISH (Book #4)
LET HER LIVE (Book #5)

DAISY FORTUNE MYSTERY SERIES
NEED YOU (Book #1)
CLAIM YOU (Book #2)
CRAVE YOU (Book #3)
CHOOSE YOU (Book #4)
CHASE YOU (Book #5)

AMBER YOUNG MYSTERY SERIES
ABSENT PITY (Book #1)
ABSENT REMORSE (Book #2)
ABSENT FEELING (Book #3)
ABSENT MERCY (Book #4)
ABSENT REASON (Book #5)

CAMI LARK MYSTERY SERIES
JUST ME (Book #1)
JUST OUTSIDE (Book #2)
JUST RIGHT (Book #3)
JUST FORGET (Book #4)
JUST ONCE (Book #5)
JUST HIDE (Book #6)

JUST NOW (Book #7)
JUST HOPE (Book #8)

NICKY LYONS MYSTERY SERIES
ALL MINE (Book #1)
ALL HIS (Book #2)
ALL HE SEES (Book #3)
ALL ALONE (Book #4)
ALL FOR ONE (Book #5)
ALL HE TAKES (Book #6)
ALL FOR ME (Book #7)
ALL IN (Book #8)

CORA SHIELDS MYSTERY SERIES
UNDONE (Book #1)
UNWANTED (Book #2)
UNHINGED (Book #3)
UNSAID (Book #4)
UNGLUED (Book #5)
UNSTABLE (Book #6)
UNKNOWN (Book #7)
UNAWARE (Book #8)

MAY MOORE SUSPENSE THRILLER
NEVER RUN (Book #1)
NEVER TELL (Book #2)
NEVER LIVE (Book #3)
NEVER HIDE (Book #4)
NEVER FORGIVE (Book #5)
NEVER AGAIN (Book #6)
NEVER LOOK BACK (Book #7)
NEVER FORGET (Book #8)
NEVER LET GO (Book #9)
NEVER PRETEND (Book #10)
NEVER HESITATE (Book #11)

PAIGE KING MYSTERY SERIES
THE GIRL HE PINED (Book #1)
THE GIRL HE CHOSE (Book #2)
THE GIRL HE TOOK (Book #3)

THE GIRL HE WISHED (Book #4)
THE GIRL HE CROWNED (Book #5)
THE GIRL HE WATCHED (Book #6)
THE GIRL HE WANTED (Book #7)
THE GIRL HE CLAIMED (Book #8)

VALERIE LAW MYSTERY SERIES
NO MERCY (Book #1)
NO PITY (Book #2)
NO FEAR (Book #3)
NO SLEEP (Book #4)
NO QUARTER (Book #5)
NO CHANCE (Book #6)
NO REFUGE (Book #7)
NO GRACE (Book #8)
NO ESCAPE (Book #9)

RACHEL GIFT MYSTERY SERIES
HER LAST WISH (Book #1)
HER LAST CHANCE (Book #2)
HER LAST HOPE (Book #3)
HER LAST FEAR (Book #4)
HER LAST CHOICE (Book #5)
HER LAST BREATH (Book #6)
HER LAST MISTAKE (Book #7)
HER LAST DESIRE (Book #8)
HER LAST REGRET (Book #9)
HER LAST HOUR (Book #10)

AVA GOLD MYSTERY SERIES
CITY OF PREY (Book #1)
CITY OF FEAR (Book #2)
CITY OF BONES (Book #3)
CITY OF GHOSTS (Book #4)
CITY OF DEATH (Book #5)
CITY OF VICE (Book #6)

A YEAR IN EUROPE
A MURDER IN PARIS (Book #1)
DEATH IN FLORENCE (Book #2)

VENGEANCE IN VIENNA (Book #3)
A FATALITY IN SPAIN (Book #4)

ELLA DARK FBI SUSPENSE THRILLER
GIRL, ALONE (Book #1)
GIRL, TAKEN (Book #2)
GIRL, HUNTED (Book #3)
GIRL, SILENCED (Book #4)
GIRL, VANISHED (Book 5)
GIRL ERASED (Book #6)
GIRL, FORSAKEN (Book #7)
GIRL, TRAPPED (Book #8)
GIRL, EXPENDABLE (Book #9)
GIRL, ESCAPED (Book #10)
GIRL, HIS (Book #11)
GIRL, LURED (Book #12)
GIRL, MISSING (Book #13)
GIRL, UNKNOWN (Book #14)

LAURA FROST FBI SUSPENSE THRILLER
ALREADY GONE (Book #1)
ALREADY SEEN (Book #2)
ALREADY TRAPPED (Book #3)
ALREADY MISSING (Book #4)
ALREADY DEAD (Book #5)
ALREADY TAKEN (Book #6)
ALREADY CHOSEN (Book #7)
ALREADY LOST (Book #8)
ALREADY HIS (Book #9)
ALREADY LURED (Book #10)
ALREADY COLD (Book #11)

EUROPEAN VOYAGE COZY MYSTERY SERIES
MURDER (AND BAKLAVA) (Book #1)
DEATH (AND APPLE STRUDEL) (Book #2)
CRIME (AND LAGER) (Book #3)
MISFORTUNE (AND GOUDA) (Book #4)
CALAMITY (AND A DANISH) (Book #5)
MAYHEM (AND HERRING) (Book #6)

ADELE SHARP MYSTERY SERIES
LEFT TO DIE (Book #1)
LEFT TO RUN (Book #2)
LEFT TO HIDE (Book #3)
LEFT TO KILL (Book #4)
LEFT TO MURDER (Book #5)
LEFT TO ENVY (Book #6)
LEFT TO LAPSE (Book #7)
LEFT TO VANISH (Book #8)
LEFT TO HUNT (Book #9)
LEFT TO FEAR (Book #10)
LEFT TO PREY (Book #11)
LEFT TO LURE (Book #12)
LEFT TO CRAVE (Book #13)
LEFT TO LOATHE (Book #14)
LEFT TO HARM (Book #15)
LEFT TO RUIN (Book #16)

THE AU PAIR SERIES
ALMOST GONE (Book#1)
ALMOST LOST (Book #2)
ALMOST DEAD (Book #3)

ZOE PRIME MYSTERY SERIES
FACE OF DEATH (Book#1)
FACE OF MURDER (Book #2)
FACE OF FEAR (Book #3)
FACE OF MADNESS (Book #4)
FACE OF FURY (Book #5)
FACE OF DARKNESS (Book #6)

A JESSIE HUNT PSYCHOLOGICAL SUSPENSE SERIES
THE PERFECT WIFE (Book #1)
THE PERFECT BLOCK (Book #2)
THE PERFECT HOUSE (Book #3)
THE PERFECT SMILE (Book #4)
THE PERFECT LIE (Book #5)
THE PERFECT LOOK (Book #6)
THE PERFECT AFFAIR (Book #7)
THE PERFECT ALIBI (Book #8)

THE PERFECT NEIGHBOR (Book #9)
THE PERFECT DISGUISE (Book #10)
THE PERFECT SECRET (Book #11)
THE PERFECT FAÇADE (Book #12)
THE PERFECT IMPRESSION (Book #13)
THE PERFECT DECEIT (Book #14)
THE PERFECT MISTRESS (Book #15)
THE PERFECT IMAGE (Book #16)
THE PERFECT VEIL (Book #17)
THE PERFECT INDISCRETION (Book #18)
THE PERFECT RUMOR (Book #19)
THE PERFECT COUPLE (Book #20)
THE PERFECT MURDER (Book #21)
THE PERFECT HUSBAND (Book #22)
THE PERFECT SCANDAL (Book #23)
THE PERFECT MASK (Book #24)
THE PERFECT RUSE (Book #25)
THE PERFECT VENEER (Book #26)
THE PERFECT PEOPLE (Book #27)
THE PERFECT WITNESS (Book #28)

CHLOE FINE PSYCHOLOGICAL SUSPENSE SERIES
NEXT DOOR (Book #1)
A NEIGHBOR'S LIE (Book #2)
CUL DE SAC (Book #3)
SILENT NEIGHBOR (Book #4)
HOMECOMING (Book #5)
TINTED WINDOWS (Book #6)

KATE WISE MYSTERY SERIES
IF SHE KNEW (Book #1)
IF SHE SAW (Book #2)
IF SHE RAN (Book #3)
IF SHE HID (Book #4)
IF SHE FLED (Book #5)
IF SHE FEARED (Book #6)
IF SHE HEARD (Book #7)

THE MAKING OF RILEY PAIGE SERIES
WATCHING (Book #1)

WAITING (Book #2)
LURING (Book #3)
TAKING (Book #4)
STALKING (Book #5)
KILLING (Book #6)

RILEY PAIGE MYSTERY SERIES
ONCE GONE (Book #1)
ONCE TAKEN (Book #2)
ONCE CRAVED (Book #3)
ONCE LURED (Book #4)
ONCE HUNTED (Book #5)
ONCE PINED (Book #6)
ONCE FORSAKEN (Book #7)
ONCE COLD (Book #8)
ONCE STALKED (Book #9)
ONCE LOST (Book #10)
ONCE BURIED (Book #11)
ONCE BOUND (Book #12)
ONCE TRAPPED (Book #13)
ONCE DORMANT (Book #14)
ONCE SHUNNED (Book #15)
ONCE MISSED (Book #16)
ONCE CHOSEN (Book #17)

MACKENZIE WHITE MYSTERY SERIES
BEFORE HE KILLS (Book #1)
BEFORE HE SEES (Book #2)
BEFORE HE COVETS (Book #3)
BEFORE HE TAKES (Book #4)
BEFORE HE NEEDS (Book #5)
BEFORE HE FEELS (Book #6)
BEFORE HE SINS (Book #7)
BEFORE HE HUNTS (Book #8)
BEFORE HE PREYS (Book #9)
BEFORE HE LONGS (Book #10)
BEFORE HE LAPSES (Book #11)
BEFORE HE ENVIES (Book #12)
BEFORE HE STALKS (Book #13)
BEFORE HE HARMS (Book #14)

AVERY BLACK MYSTERY SERIES
CAUSE TO KILL (Book #1)
CAUSE TO RUN (Book #2)
CAUSE TO HIDE (Book #3)
CAUSE TO FEAR (Book #4)
CAUSE TO SAVE (Book #5)
CAUSE TO DREAD (Book #6)

KERI LOCKE MYSTERY SERIES
A TRACE OF DEATH (Book #1)
A TRACE OF MURDER (Book #2)
A TRACE OF VICE (Book #3)
A TRACE OF CRIME (Book #4)
A TRACE OF HOPE (Book #5)

Made in the USA
Las Vegas, NV
19 June 2025

23779630R00090